The Strength of Weeds

M. M. Blyth

For Todd.

Thank you for teaching us

what matters in life.

"You know those plants that are always trying to find the light?

Maybe they were planted in a location that didn't necessarily

facilitate growth, but inexplicably they make a circuitous route

to not only survive but bloom into a beautiful plant."

- Jonathan Van Ness

"They say it's my fault she's gone."

My mama died.

Don't worry, it was a long time ago. Almost ten years before this story starts, when she was having me. Pop says she lived long enough to give me lots of kisses and a name, and then she closed her eyes forever.

Mama picked the names for all of us kids. Their relationship was give and take in that way. In our parts, it isn't too common for the woman to choose the names - that was considered the man's task. But Pops didn't mind one bit. Despite him being the biggest person on our side of the bayou, he has the heart and soul of a newborn fawn. Unless he's playing the spoons or the washboard he tends to be a wallflower, watching us from the sidelines and gently smiling beneath his scruffy beard.

She loved to garden, and named all six of us in that way. Rose is the oldest at nearly seventeen, the only girl besides me, and the whole reason I'm telling this story in the first place. She's just like a rose, too. Beautiful, gentle, delicate. She is the spitting image of Mama, and me of Pops, but we have the same eyes. A pre-thunderstorm grey, full of clouds and fog.

And next come the boys, all four of them right in a row: Reed, Evergreen, who goes by Ever, Fern, and Ash. If they weren't a few inches apart in height, you would have an impossible time telling one from the other. If us girls have eyes like the sky, then the boys have the surrounding land. Mischievous and playful, forest green glints out from under each of their shaggy brows. They got the most beautiful mix of Mama's creamy vanilla skin and Pop's deep olive complexion. Thick waves of dark auburn hair, the same shade as our fertile soil, shake and bounce when they run across the yard playing tag.

And then there's me, Ivy. Pop says that if I had been a boy, Mama was going to call me Oak. I sure am glad I'm a girl, because Oak just doesn't seem like it would work for me. Just like Rose perfectly fits into her name, I think you'll find that I have grown into Ivy, too.

****

We live in Solitaire, a tiny community of towering cypresses and one-room shanties about a mile east of the bayou. I've never seen it on a map, and the only visitors we get are down-on-their-luck relatives looking for a roof to cover their heads. When the country nearly fell apart a few years ago in '29, the government set up a bunch of these neighborhoods. They were supposed to be a means for families to have an opportunity at working in the nearby mines. New trains and cars needed coal more than ever, so the demand for labor was a much-needed welcome. I guess some parts of the U.S. have gotten better since then, but we don't know anything about that.

I'm not sure how many of us live around here exactly. There's the seven of us, then there's Crazy David and his big old coon hound Sylvia. Their shack is about a ten minute walk from ours and you pass by it whenever you make the long trek into town. He's mostly nice, but if he catches you and starts talking, you're looking at a thirty minute conversation, if you're lucky. Everyone loves Sylvia though, and each evening I save a few bites of crawfish or scoops of rice to bring to her. When she's not sunning on their front porch, she's wandering around and sniffing all the rich smells the swamps have to offer.

The Mass family lives across the water on the other side of the creek and Pops says that he's grateful for the distance. I have never been able to keep track of how many kids they have, but they're all dirty and loud and even crazier than Crazy David. Sometimes Ever and I watch for big gators coming up their side of the bank and cross our fingers. A few more folks live nearby, all of us occupying nearly identical ramshackle homes. Some more filled with love than others. When all of Solitaire gets together for crawfish boils I would guess there are about forty of us in total.

Of all the homes in all of Louisiana, I would bet my only pair of shoes that ours has the most life and energy. It's almost like when Mama died, Pop took it upon himself to love us all double. And while our bellies sometimes rumble with emptiness, our hearts are always filled to the brim. On Sundays, when all the boys get to stay home from work, we play stickball on the flat grassy patch outside our front porch, and go fishing for Bluegills in the weed beds off of the bayou. Pop builds billowing fires and we roast wild pecans and hazelnuts. Ever and Fern play rusty tunes on our grandpa's old banjo while the rest of us sing and dance around the crackling flames.

But it's not always happy. Some of the older folks around here tell me to be more like my sister, that my mama would be ashamed to see me now. One time, mean old Mrs. Adur from church looked me right in the face and told me so.

"Your mother must be turnin' in her grave with you runnin' around like a little hoodlum," she sneered. "It's a good thing her memories of a daughter were of Rose and not you."

My chest felt like it was made of concrete, like it couldn't breathe after hearing those poisonous words. I wanted to scream and shout at her that my mama thinks I'm wonderful. That we talk everyday and she shows me how much she loves me. Maybe if I could have stayed calm, bit my tongue and explained myself, I would have changed her mind. Unfortunately, as you may come to discover, that is rarely in the cards for me. Instead, I exploded.

"Oh yeah?" I shouted, shoving my finger into her ancient, wrinkled shoulder. "Well no one likes you because you smell like bird poo and look like a dinosaur!" Reed grabbed me from behind and dragged me home, hollering apologies over my insult-laden rantings.

Thankfully, Pops doesn't get mad at me for feeling the way I feel or speaking my mind. Later that night, after a dinner of freshly caught, salt-fried catfish and okra, he pulled me aside and we walked past our garden and front yard to the edge of the water. It was such a clear night that the entire Milky Way shone down on us. Peering up at Orion, he crouched next to me and whispered, "You know what baby? Roses are beautiful and everybody loves 'em, but they need special care and attention." He stroked my tight curls, vining around his fingers, and wiped away the huge, silent tears tumbling over my freckled cheeks.

"But ivy? Ivy grows anywhere without anyone's help. Ivy don't need nobody. Ivy takes over everything else in the area and can't be destroyed. The only thing ivy needs is a little water and some sun, and you can't stop it."

I don't think the other folks are mean on purpose. They all really loved my mama and miss her lots, so when they see me they think about her dying. They say it's my fault she's gone. But I know my mama wanted to hang on and be with all of us here. Her poor body was just too tired and wouldn't let her keep going. I hear she was like her name, too; Lily.

Sometimes I wonder if she knew she wasn't going to make it. Sometimes, I think she named me Ivy on purpose, to give me the strength to keep going.

"I'm good at knowing when I don't know something."

"You can't pick the carrots yet, I. They're not done growin'."

"That's what you think - taste 'em now and tell me they ain't better like this."

Rose shook the earth off of the baby carrot I had just pulled, took a bite, and giggled. She reached both arms into the air the way the old ladies do at church, then rolled back into the cool, crisp grass. A belly laugh roared out of me as she sat back up and started pulling a bunch more out of the ground, her thick golden waves flowing down over her shoulders.

"I don't know why I'm the big sister but you're wiser than me," she teased.

"Age is only a number," I said in my best impression of Pop's gruffy voice.

Laughing and wiping my dirty hands on the front of my overalls, I headed inside to start washing up for supper. My hair pushed itself into my eyes again and I grabbed an old piece of ribbon to tie back my unruly locks. Pops tried to help me tackle my ringlets a few weeks ago, but all he did was give me a hack job. Each time we thought he was done, he would take a step back and say, "Hm...I think it's a little too long on the left." So he would shorten it up, but then the right would be too long. When it was all said and done, my rust-colored curls sat at my shoulders in some places and closer to my ears in others, and I was too traumatized to let anyone else try to fix it. I can only imagine that my new style furthered some neighbors' colorful opinions of me.

Through the screen door and splintered walls, Rose's voice carried across the garden and into our little home. She was singing an old favorite, *Sun of my Soul.* When Pop was around they would harmonize together, sending all of us into a dreamy state, happily nodding along. Rose has always seen the good parts about me, like Mama would have, and that part of the day was my favorite. When it was just us girls getting ready for the boys to come home, our daily chores and housework done, only dinner to prepare. When the thick heat of the day starts to creep away and the crickets begin to make their presence known. When the breeze off the creek starts tickling our skin, blowing off some of the day's hard work.

Our wash bin was rusted through the bottom in so many parts that it wouldn't hold water on its own anymore. Pop had tried to fix it with some lumber scraps, but those rotted through quicker than a bullfrog catches a fly. We all teased Ash when he suggested putting a thick layer of sand at the bottom, but it has actually been the best solution so far. We can always tell who cleaned the plates, though. If I did it, someone inevitably finds a few grainy bites in their dinner.

The carrots were rinsed and I examined our meager pantry shelf for something that would resemble a full meal. Twice a month, I head into town with a few dollars of the mine money to get some canned food and dried beans. Every once in a while we have enough for a fresh chicken, and nothing brings more joy to the Green family! When that happens, Pops gets so excited that he dances around and squawks like a big fat rooster, all of us joining in like his crazed chicklets. We call it the Pop-A-Doodle-Do. If anyone ever saw us in that state, they would probably consider sending us to a government agency, but we always thought it was hilarious. Unfortunately, we haven't gotten to do our funny little dance in a long time. And the last time I went to town was over three weeks ago. With a heavy sigh, I threw our last handfuls of black eyed peas into a pot of boiling water and decided to check the crawfish traps. I knew we needed those little guys, I knew how much we relied on and appreciated them, but I hated checking those cages. I always felt so guilty pulling a full trap out of the water.

"Ivy!" Rose called from the back garden, "Will you look down the path? I hear someone comin'!"

My brows furrowed. It's strange to hear voices on the path during the day since all the men are in the mines or fields and all the ladies are at home keeping life going. I pressed my face against the biggest crack in our wall, a gap between two of the wall boards above the boys' mattress, and saw Pops and the boys coming home a full three hours early. Nothing to fret over, it was just them.

"Don't worry!" I called back. "It's just the boys!"

Rose didn't respond, so I shouted louder. "It's just the guys, Rose!" Still nothing. I headed out back again to tell her closer, but when I turned the corner I could tell that she had heard me the first time. Her face was real light, like my summertime dress looked when I first got it, and the tomatoes in her hands slipped down to the ground, slowly rolling in the dirt. A quiet panic filled my body. Why would she react that way? Without saying a word, she turned and walked towards Pop. Long, urgent strides.

I'm good at knowing when I don't know something and this was one of those times. I watched her rush towards the boys, tense and focused, then gathered the tomatoes and went inside to start supper by myself. My uneasiness stretched across our one-room home.

My stomach flipped around as I stoked the fire under our pot of beans. Steadying my hand, I reached for our sharpest knife, coining carrots and tossing them into the pot. It must have only been a few minutes, but it felt like an entire day had passed by the time I heard my family's voices through the screen door. The boys came bounding in, moving like a new species of creature with one brain, eight legs, and eight arms. They have always been a pack like that, hardly more than a few feet away from each other at any given time. My brothers not only shared a home, they shared a mattress and a job. They collapsed on the sagging plywood floor and started their daily routine of peeling off the long johns they wore to stay cool in the mines. As the pile of dusty cotton grows, I carry it all outside to smack off as much coal as possible. Every night after dinner, I boil them over the outside fire pit, then string them up to dry overnight. Even though he was the third youngest, Fern was the smallest of all of us on account of being born too soon. The long johns we had for him were still so big that he had to fold the cuffs at least three times. Reed, on the other hand, was getting so big each day that he could almost beat Pops in a wrestling match. Almost.

The charcoal from years of hard labor was so worn into their fingers and scalps that the wash bin was a waste of time. Instead, they would just jump into the creek that flowed out of the bayou. Sometimes I joined in and Ash would hoist me onto his shoulders so that we could play Chicken against

Fern and Reed. Ever and Rose always watched from the bank, too mature to fight with any of us, even if it was all in good fun.

"Where are Rose and Pop? She ok?" I asked, knowing which one would respond.

More boots thumping the ground, more socks piling up in the corner.

"Pops is real bad, I," muttered Reed, always the first to answer. "They're closin' down the mine."

I turned to face them and stared hard at my oldest brother. My head felt heavy and light all at the same time, like it might split in half if I let it. That mine was our whole wide everything. What would we do without it? Maybe that's why I hadn't been to the store in so long. Had there already been problems with the mine and I just hadn't noticed? Was I so focused on each day that I hadn't seen the bigger picture unraveling in front of me? Ever and Ash finished changing and shuffled over to help me cut up the carrots. I started chopping the tomatoes so we could have some sauce to cook the crawdads in.

"Well how much more time do we have until the mine closes?" I wondered aloud. "Me and Rose can look for new jobs for you until then."

Reed sighed real loud and heavy, then threw the carrots down and left. Ever shook his head and took a deep breath. He was always the gentlest, a sweet old grandpa inhabiting a teenage boy's body.

"Ivy, it's closed. Now. That's why we're home early," he lamented. "And, it's lookin' like we won't even get our fair pay from last week's work.

The door opened with a sore, corroded creak, sounding louder than it did this morning. Pops shuffled in and sat on the boys' straw mattress, but Rose wasn't with him. He joined in on the daily process of stripping off his many layers, soot and sweat falling away from every part of him.

"Hey my little weed," he greeted me with his deep, raspy voice. He sounded both tired and panicked somehow. His back sloped down, mimicking the sad frown of his mouth. I can sense when people aren't including me just because I'm the youngest, and nothing makes me feel more frustrated and patronized. I watch them move in and out of each day. I listen to the way they say certain words, the way their shoulders hunch over when they tie their shoes. I can feel what's going on even if I don't know the exact details. Why couldn't they realize that? All I wanted was to be included in the conversation. My fear morphed into anger with every second that passed.

"Where's Rose and what's going on?" I demanded, tired of being kept in the dark.

"Ivy, we gotta talk about somethin' real important."

"What's going on?!" I yelled it this time.

"Dammit Ivy!" Pops bellowed in response, throwing one of his big work boots he had been taking off. He pinched his nose between his eyes and took a slow, deep breath. Pops never gets angry with us, and he sure as heck had never thrown a boot across the room before. My heart pounded and I suddenly felt prickly tears building up behind my eyes.

"She's fine. She's in the garden. Will you be quiet for a second and listen without interruptin'?"

He exhaled, pushing out all the air he had in him, and leaned forward so that his elbows were propped on his knees.

"Ivy, your sister is getting older," he paused for a long time, rubbing his forehead. The boys leaned up against the wall, staring blankly ahead or down at their bare feet, like they were waiting for their sentences.

"And even though times have changed since I was her age," he continued, "there are some ways of doing things the old fashioned way that are as good as ever. My sister did it, and your Uncle Chester did it, too." He bit the side of his thumb and looked down at the dirty laundry at his feet.

"It's already been real hard to get enough food for all seven of us, right? But with the mine closed down it's gonna be impossible." He stopped again, this time looking up at the ceiling like he could see the clouds behind it. Like the whole sky was there with him, just him and the heavens. And then he came back to Earth. "It's about time we find a husband for Rose."

****

You know that sensation when all your blood whooshes up from your feet to your head? Like when you fluctuate between hot and cold at the same time and you burst into an instant sweat? My brain was stuck between asleep and awake, not sure where to go or what to do. Our splintered walls contracted around me, getting ready to implode. Living without Rose was the most terrifying, heartbreaking nightmare that had ever crossed my mind. I had so many thoughts bumping into each other in my head that I couldn't even say anything. It felt impossible.

My fingers clenched up and tightened around the tomato still locked in my hand, echoing the chaos in my mind. Without even thinking about it, I threw that tomato as hard as I could, right at my father. It hit him square in the chin and exploded all over his face and neck, shiny seeds and runny juice dripping off of his beard. Then I stomped on his foot as hard as I could and took off running.

"If it's the smart thing to do, then it's the right thing to do."

A few years ago, when I was six or seven, we were on our way home from town after a few good weeks in the mine. We were able to buy so many beans and bags of grits that our flour sacks were too full to pull shut. Rose was able to carry hers on her back, but I had to take some breaks and sometimes drag mine down the dusty road. We couldn't wait to surprise Pops and the boys with a roast chicken and baked beans when they got home. The whole walk back, we planned out our meal; Rose would start the fire and season the chicken, and I would put together the spices for the beans. We have always been like two bodies with one mind when we're in the kitchen together. When we turned around the bend into Solitaire, our eyes fell on a random rock in the middle of the path. A perfectly flat, round, shiny green rock. It most certainly hadn't been there on our way out and we hadn't seen anyone else on the path. We both stopped in our tracks and stared.

"I think it's a magic rock," I whispered to Rose. Her elbow prodded my ribs and she rolled her eyes. "No I'm serious," I protested. "How did it get here? I think it has powers."
I paused. "Let's take it home."

"Look at how much stuff we already have! We can't lug that home, too," Rose answered. But I was determined. I put my flour sack on top of that damn rock and, squatting down and scooting backwards, slowly pulled the whole mess home. My butt was sore for a week afterwards.

Over time I realized that the rock wasn't actually magic, but we both still loved it and laughed at my stubbornness whenever we saw it. It lived between two of mama's big purple hydrangea bushes now, and Rose was perched on top of it. Even if Pops hadn't mentioned it, I knew she would be in the garden. I knew where she would be and how she would be sitting. I knew the look that would be on her face, and how her dress would be folded between her knees.

"You ok?" I asked when I first got a glimpse of her yellow hem through the blooms. She shrugged her shoulders, eyes fixed on the ground. I know that vulnerable place of not wanting to talk, but not wanting to be alone, so I didn't say anything and just sat down next to her. Dragonflies flew all around us, flitting in and out with their iridescent, windowpane wings, landing on a leaf and then taking off again right away. I wished that I could fly away.

Cricket chirps rose all around us and a warm breeze came off of the water, brushing my cheek. "You don't have to do this ya know," I pleaded in Rose's direction. My jaw felt tight and sore.

Nothing happened for a while. I listened to the leaves rustle around us, and eventually I could hear Rose's breath going up and down, a quiet drum keeping the rhythm between us. The branches shifted as she stretched her legs out straight in front of her.

"If it's the smart thing to do, then it's the right thing to do," she reassured me, looking down at one of the dragonflies perched next to her. Hearing

Rose speak so casually about leaving us was more hurtful than old Mrs. Adur.

"Smart?" I blurted out. "What's so smart about moving in with some stranger?" My body stiffened and I shot up so that I was standing over her. I must have raised my voice too, because Reed peeked out of the front door. I didn't care. I wanted him to hear me. Why wasn't anyone else mad about this?

"Is it smart to abandon your baby sister?" I screamed out. Rose looked up at me, then nodded and managed a sad smile. A long pause filled the air.

"If leavin' you means that you'll be fed, I won't think twice about it." Guilt and despair coursed through my veins.

Reed stepped towards the garden. "Ivy, come on in and have some supper. You must be starvin'," he called. I knew he was trying to help, but the only help I wanted was for someone to help me stop all this. I would rather starve than have Rose leave us.

"I'll eat when my family decides they haven't lost their minds and won't be sellin' my sister," I protested, not taking my eyes off of her. I wanted her to know that I would never, ever, sit by while something bad happened to her.

"What?" he cocked his head to the side.

"You heard me," I crossed my arms.

Reed didn't know what to do with this new information, but Rose actually let out a small chuckle.

"Are...are you goin' on a hunger strike?" he stammered, scratching his thick curls.

"Damn straight." I clenched my teeth and fists and turned to look at my brother.

He would never have to fear what was happening to Rose, so he had no real way of understanding. It wasn't his fault. It wasn't even Pop's fault. It was just a bad part of life.

"Sometimes, I wish she'd named you Thistle."

I slept in the garden. My anger was too great to fit inside that night. Outside, I could clench my fists and kick the ground without anyone trying to fix me or tell me to calm down. Not even Rose was safe from my wrath. Why wasn't she fighting this? I just wanted someone to feel the way I felt. I didn't want anyone to tell me it would be alright, to try and hush me. I just wanted someone to stand next to me and say 'You're right, this is horrible and I'm so sorry.' I wanted someone to let me feel the way I was feeling without saying it was wrong. The deep, dark sky was my only companion that night. Its stars twirled and twinkled, reminding me of how little I was.

Sometimes, when it seems like the pieces of my life aren't fitting together quite right, like it's swirling all around without my control, I pretend I'm a queen. I figure that's how queens probably live, managing a million things at once. If they run a kingdom filled with other people, some of which probably hate them, there is bound to be a lot of mess they have to deal with. Don't you think? There must be endless problems they have to sort through, and yet they have to make it look easy and graceful. I think queens might have the hardest jobs in the whole wide world. When we were little, I used to make crowns out of twigs and braided wildflowers and march around with it. I'm too old for that bit now, but sometimes I still imagine that I'm wearing a crown. On days like that, when nothing seems to be going right, I ask myself, 'What would a queen do?'

I also told a bit of a fib. When I'm hungry I fall apart real fast, but I pledged that I wouldn't eat until Pops came to his senses. Sleeping in the garden made it easier to sneak some carrots and cucumbers. A queen has to do what a queen has to do.

The door's familiar, grouchy greeting sounded early, followed by Rose's voice humming *Ave Maria*. I always thought that was her most beautiful song. Peeking through some fence slats, I saw her heading down to the well, apron on and wash bin in hand. Even after her family betrayed her she was still taking care of them. I set my mind right then that I would live in the garden until Pops came out and explained how he was wrong. Even if it took a whole week, I didn't care. I was certain that he would realize it at some point.

******

The sun was high above and a deep, endless heat had attached itself to anything and everything nearby. Even the towering oak trees seemed to be wilting. My cool, fresh garden hotel had converted itself into a stuffy sauna, and I had neared my breaking point when I heard Pops coming around the side of the garden. Wanting to look as pitiful as possible so that he would have to listen to me, I mussed up my hair some more and rubbed dirt across my face. My rusty cheeks were now covered in dirt freckles, adding to the crowd that permanently dotted my nose. As I waited for him to come around to me, I stared straight ahead, pretending that I didn't even notice him. His boots came scuffling up to the hydrangea bushes, kicking up dust and old flower petals as he got closer.

"Sometimes, I wish she'd named you Thistle," he teased, and I could hear that he was smiling. "You know what thistle is, right?" He asked me, his gravelly voice making me feel more comfortable. I kept looking past him.

"It's this little flower that looks like it's made out of clouds. It's light and airy, and if a breeze comes it just blows away. Taken by the wind."

He kneeled down across from me, coming to my level. "But you ain't that. You're my tough little weed. Ain't no one gonna push you around. Even me." My eyes darted towards him for a second, so I turned my head to look the other way. He adjusted, sitting cross-legged in front of me. This bush I had used as a motel for the night suddenly looked like a tiny little herb.

"Ivy, your mama knew all six of you in a way that I never could."

I looked up at him for the first time, but he was fiddling with a twig. My eyes darted back down. "I wish I had some of her insight, but I don't." He cleared his throat. "Please just listen to me," he pleaded. His eyes looked just like Rose's did yesterday - wide, scared.

"I don't know what to do, I. Short of lettin' everybody slowly starve to death." He settled back further into his seat and rubbed his temples.

"Do you remember how we had a few more crawfish boils this spring and there were new fellas comin' to join us?" I hadn't thought about that being anything out of the ordinary at that point.

"Yeah, I remember," I pouted at him.

"Well that was the first try," he answered. "The first try at findin' a suitor for Rose. When that didn't stick, she brought up this idea a few weeks back, when we first heard a rumor of the mines closin'."

I felt like I had been kicked in the stomach. This was Rose's idea? She wanted to leave? They all knew this might happen and didn't tell me? My bottom lip started to quiver.

"You know that she loves us so much," he continued, "and that she would do anything in the world for us, especially you. She's like your mama like that."

As disappointed and heartbroken as I was, it all made sense now. Pops would never ask Rose to do this, but she would do it for us. She really was just like Mama. She didn't want to leave us, but she knew it was her time to go.

"You don't have to say anything, but I hope you join us for supper later. Me and the boys are cookin', and I'd rather not have people askin' me 'bout a hunger strike in my own home."

He patted me on the head, then turned away from me to head back inside. I know he didn't mean to, but when he ruffled my hair he knocked off my crown.

"You're the version of her she always wanted to be."

The afternoon heat broke wide open, sending the bullfrogs deep into their lily pad caves. Even the gulls, always with something on their minds, took a momentary vow of silence. My conviction to stay outside dwindled as the day droned on and I mentally surrendered, deciding to come back inside for supper. But I wasn't ready to see anyone just yet. My feelings were still so upside-down and inside-out that I needed more time and a new setting to clear my mind. It takes awhile for the boys to cook, so I decided to head down our dirt path. There was only one person whose company sounded appealing to me, and I knew I had the time to get there.

Miss Mavis is older than rocks. I think she may have been alive when Louisiana was still France, and her house was definitely around then. Her family has been in the area for generations; her four greats grandpa was a fur-trapper from Europe and had settled in way back then. One of those grandpas built her house and her family has lived in it ever since. Now it is just Miss Mavis, her only daughter grown and gone, somewhere in the North. Her driveway is so long and twisty that you can't even see the house when you stand at the end of it, but as you stroll down the canopied walkway with ferns and wildflowers lining the edges, eventually the two-story white colonial greets you. A set of rocking chairs sits on the wraparound porch and black shutters frame each window, blinking open and closed depending on the heat of the day. Shiny wood floors run through the whole bottom floor, and the kitchen always smells like fresh cookies. Miss Mavis might just be my best friend, and I think I might be hers, too.

It takes a good hour and change to walk there, but since I didn't need to worry about fixing dinner, I had the time. I have made that trip every Sunday afternoon for as long as I can remember. But since it was only Tuesday, it would be a surprise. Before my weekly trips ever started, my mama walked that route every day for years and years. I loved picturing her strolling down the same path I was on. What did she think about with all that time on her hands? Did she admire the cypress trees like I did? Had she taken the same shortcut?

Mama grew up in New Orleans, the daughter of a local tailor and seamstress, but unexpectedly moved to the country with her sisters after their parents died from tuberculosis. Not knowing what to do, but unafraid of hard work, she roamed around looking for any job she could think of. She landed upon Miss Mavis's house and offered to do anything useful - clean, garden, sew, cook. Miss Mavis was grateful for the help and company, and the rest is history. Or at least, it's a story for another day.

Pops, on the other hand, was born and raised in Solitaire. His grandparents were Greek immigrants who made the dangerous journey across the Atlantic in pursuit of a better life, nothing more than the clothes on their back. Coming from a rural fishing town in Greece, Pop says they had a hard time adjusting to life in New York. When some southern states started campaigns to bring immigrants down to work as sharecroppers, they took the chance. Unaware of the challenges that would bring, they packed up their few belongings and headed to Louisiana. After seven years of stripping sugar cane on a plantation, they purchased their freedom and bought the small plot of land we live on today. My gramps was a good fisherman, and he made enough money to get by selling and trading at the local markets and swap meets. They were too old to fight the Spanish flu when it came through, and ever since then it was just us.

As my bare feet thudded along and the rolled bottoms of my tattered overalls collected more dust, I forced myself to try and think differently about all this. To consider it like I was someone else, not Ivy. If it was her idea, maybe Rose leaving wasn't such a horrifying idea. Maybe she actually wanted to leave and start something new. Maybe I was just being selfish and making her feel bad.

****

There is a shortcut to Miss Mavis's that no one knows about except me. Off the dirt road, an ancient old willow tree guards it like a weathered sentry. When you gently part its long braids and peek below, you see a cool, clear creek with lots of white and purple lilies. If you cross over the water instead of staying on the road, you save a good count to a thousand. And it's not a fast, deep creek unless it's flooding season. If you're not wearing shoes and you pick up your dress or roll your bottoms up to your knees, you can just walk straight across with only your skin getting wet. I like it because it's quick and refreshing during a summer day. Plus, I get to smell my mama's flowers.

The events of the past twenty four hours, coupled with true Louisiana summer heat, made me look like a feral orphan by the time I arrived at

Miss Mavis's. I tried real hard to brush the dirt off the knees of my overalls and smoosh my hair down, but it was no use. While Rose had beautiful, shiny waves, I got stuck with tiny, frizzy ringlets that often resembled a copper bird's nest. Twigs sometimes included. I licked my palms to press down my part and knocked on the door.

When someone is hogging the hot sauce or taking forever to use the outhouse, Pops tells us, 'Patience is waiting with a smile.' So, I waited real patiently and plastered on a big grin since Miss Mavis is so darn old and it takes her a long time to move. I went over how to tell her about what was going on, and then decided to just keep my big mouth shut until she asked. She would help me figure it all out. Footsteps shuffled on the other side of the door, and the little bell attached to the top began twinkling as I watched it pull away from me.

"Well if it isn't Miss Ivy Green!" she beamed, her fluffy white hair pulled up into a bun.

"To what do I owe this most pleasant surprise?" Miss Mavis cupped my face in both of her soft, wrinkled hands and I smiled despite myself.

"Come on in my child," she beckoned, leading me down her hallway and into the kitchen where she started some tea. Even though she hadn't been expecting company, she was still dressed in a pretty yellow skirt with white birds all over it, wings outstretched in flight. Her chubby, loveable beagle lay snoring on a pillow in the corner. "Hi Molly," I whispered to her with a soft pat on the head.

"Well now Miss Ivy," she started. I loved the way she always called me "Miss." She had a good way of reminding me that I was pretty and important, even when I showed up unannounced and barefoot in overalls. Bustling around the kitchen, I watched as she grabbed glasses and set out snack plates.

"You've never been so quiet in all the years I've known you. Are you ok child?" she wondered. My head started swirling around again, and even though I swore that I would handle myself like a real lady, I just couldn't help it. It all came out before I even knew it had started, just like when I threw the tomato at Pop. I took a few breaths in an attempt to stave it off, but all the words blurted out like a broken dam wall in a hurricane.

"Pops can't work anymore 'cause the mines are closin' so he's afraid we're all gonna starve so we have to sell Rose to any old bum who wants to be her husband and no one is upset about it 'cept me!"

Hot tears built up in my eyes and I suddenly wished I hadn't come at all. I hate crying and I hate being embarrassed. Crying in front of Miss Mavis was about the most humiliating thing I could think of.

Her thin, whispery eyebrows pressed together, exaggerating the wrinkles on her forehead. She set down the glasses she was holding and swooped over from the other side of the kitchen to grab me up in a real big hug. It amazed me how fast and strong she was for being so old.

"Sweet child," she comforted, rocking me back and forth. Salty tears soaked through her white embroidered cardigan. "You sweet Ivy, you. You have one of my favorite souls, you know that?" And she pulled away, cupping my face again. But this time, it was all puffy and wet.

****

Miss Mavis got me a cool, wet rag and helped me wipe down my dirty, tear-stained face. The skin on the back of her hands reminded me of old paper, so old and thin it was almost see-through. Her blue veins pushed out like the tree roots down by the creek. Having someone take care of me made me feel better almost instantly.

We settled into rockers on the back porch, drinking cold sweet tea and munching on homemade snickerdoodles. Birds and squirrels flitted and chased each other all over her backyard while we watched them from our chairs. My toes grazed the ground as the seat went back and forth, and my mind drifted to when I still needed a boost to climb up into that very seat.

"Your mama is so proud of you Ivy, I just know it," she mused. My brows scrunched up and I shook my head. "I don't think so, Miss Mavis. Everybody else says the opposite. They all say she'd be embarrassed and that I should be ashamed of myself for runnin' around with no shoes like the boys."

Miss Mavis let out a huge guffaw, waving her hand around like she was swatting at a fly. "Anyone who says that didn't know your mama like I did," she declared, defiantly. "I knew Lily for fifteen years. For fifteen years she helped me take care of this place. And so much more." She put her glass down and shook her head. Her lips curled in like she was trying real hard to stop them from moving, and her eyes looked like she was seeing something that I couldn't. I didn't know until then how much she missed my mama, too.

She let out a huge sigh, looked at me, and smiled. "Your mama was so much like Rose. But, if I'm tellin' you the whole truth, she wanted so desperately to be like you, bold and unapologetic. You're the version of her that she always wanted to be. I think she left us so that she could give that to you. She knew who you'd be and she is tickled pink watchin' you everyday."

I had never heard such nice words before.

        "People should care as much as they say they do."

The freshly baked cookies were just a pile of crumbs that resembled the sawdust after Pops built our outside bench. I had been content and distracted for a moment, but now he sprang back into my mind. "I just don't understand how he is okay with all this," I thought aloud. "That's the part that makes me real mad. Why doesn't he seem upset about it?" I pinched some of the sweet sawdust into my mouth.

I knew Miss Mavis wanted to scold me for using my hands, but she nodded and took a sip of tea. "You know, child," she started, "grown-ups are funny like that." Her rocker clicked at a steady beat as she spoke. "Sometimes they care so much that they don't show it. Showin' it would be too scary." Click clack, click clack.

I twisted and turned that idea every which way that I could, but no matter how I thought about it, it made about as much sense to me as trying to catch fireflies at noon. "Miss Mavis," I replied, "with all due respect, that is about the stupidest thing I've ever heard."

She nearly spit out her tea and started slapping her leg. "Stop laughin'!" I yelled. "I'm serious!"

"Oh honey, I am not laughin' at you," she chuckled as she wiped tears from the corners of her eyes. "I actually respect every word you just said. But I simply cannot understand how the good Lord managed to fit so much into such a tiny space. He broke the mold with you."

"I'd rather break the mold than be like everyone else," I muttered, tipping my glass up to slide the ice into my mouth.

She smiled and nodded. "Cheers to that," she declared. "And," she continued, waving a finger in the air, "it's important for you to know that this type of arrangement wasn't so uncommon when your daddy was a boy. To him, this might not feel as momentous as it does to you. Arranging marriages and exchangin' dowries used to be commonplace." Click clack, click clack.

"Yeah," I sighed. "He did mention that yesterday. Still though, Pops always says how much he cares, but I feel like he isn't actin' like it right now." I rocked my seat with the same rhythm as her. "People should care as much as they say they do," I exhaled, crossing my arms across my chest.

Miss Mavis slowed her rocking and looked at me with a small, sad smile. "I couldn't agree more, Miss Ivy." Click clack.

"That's how it'll be done."

Miss Mavis gave me a bigger hug than usual and I drank in her familiar smells of cinnamon and laundry soap. She slipped two more cookies into my big side pockets, giving me a wink as I turned around to wave goodbye one more time. She validated my worries and questions, but that didn't do anything about the reality of what was about to change our family forever. I nibbled on the first cookie and tried to put my stubbornness aside for a second. My brain was starting to tell me that this was all okay, but my heart was still screaming and shouting in protest. I turned the corner at the end of Miss Mavis's driveway, and I swore I could still hear her characteristic click clack as my feet picked up the pace.

My cookies were long gone, having been devoured as soon as I left, and the dirt from the road made a small cloud around my feet each time I shuffled closer to home. A cool breeze had graciously replaced the heat of midday and I could take full, deep breaths again. It was Golden Hour. The setting sun, exhausted from a full day's work, cast amber filters on the pathway, making the dirt road look like ground cinnamon. The birds were all in bed; it was the crickets' turn to sing. Cypress trees stretched their huge limbs to make a tunnel over the walkway, like a perfect arch. It smelled like green. Right as I rounded the bend into Solitaire, where you can first get a peek of our garden, I saw Pops walking towards me.

"Hey Pop," I greeted, suddenly ashamed of myself for not saving a cookie for him. "You goin' to see Crazy David?"

"No baby, I was actually lookin' for you," he replied. His pace slowed and the gap between us started to shrink. "See there's a little bit of good news," he said, rubbing his broad hand over his head. This was it. He had finally come to his senses. My heart began to bump around inside my chest.

"Remember that quarry we were talkin' about the other day? The one just down on the other side of the bayou?" He scratched his head and kicked at a leaf stuck in the dirt. "Well, it's gonna open tomorrow." Not what I hoped for, but maybe new jobs would mean that Rose could stay.

While it sounded like great news to share, something about him seemed dark. Sad. His voice sounded like sand, and his eyes were still fixated on the ground. He looked tired. And old. I had never noticed how many little lines he had around his eyes. How many of his hairs and whiskers were grey. I thought that if I had to count them all it would take me the whole night.

He sighed and continued. "It pays just over three quarters of what the mines did, but it's a heck of a lot safer, so we got that goin' for us." Only a fraction of their old pay. No way Rose could stay. The bumping in my chest slowed, replacing itself with a sinking pit in my stomach. I inhaled Pop's scent of charcoal and tobacco, and nodded a few times to myself. "That's great, Pops."

We walked next to each other, real slow, heading back towards our little house. I couldn't stop thinking about how empty it would be once I was the only girl.

You ever fear something that's going to happen, but once you realize it's never going to change then you suddenly start to feel better? Something about acceptance, I suppose. Sometimes I wonder if we get more upset about the waiting than we do about the actual outcome.

A wave of resolve came over me as I focused on all the white whiskers peeking out of my Pop's beard. Like a small weight had been carried away from me. My thoughts were clearer, focused, and I knew what I needed to do.

"Hey Pop?"

"Hm?"

"Pop, I got a proposition for you." He chuckled.

"A proposition? From my baby weed?" He stopped walking, faced me, and squatted down to my level. "Ok, shoot. What's this proposition you got for me?"

While he found humor in the moment, I felt the exact opposite. This was not a joke and it was no laughing matter. I was making a serious proposal and he needed to agree to my terms. I lifted my chin a bit higher and straightened my crown.

"Well," my tongue was heavy as I searched for my words. I cleared my throat. "Well, if I can be the one to go with Rose, ya know, to walk with her and help her find someone. I mean, if it's me that gets to help her pick someone...someone nice and thoughtful...if it's me and Rose that go, then I think I might be ok with it."

He looked me square in the eye while I was talking, but when I finished he didn't change his expression. He just stared real strong. The lines on his forehead looked deeper than before, and I started to worry that he hadn't heard anything I had just said.

And then he started nodding his head. He nodded and nodded, then took a big, serious breath. He stood back up, grabbed my hand, and kept nodding as we walked home.

"Ok," he stated. "That's how it'll be done."

I felt like a million butterflies were trying to escape my stomach through my throat. It really was happening.

"Ivy girl," Pops remarked after a minute. "You know it's not 'me and Rose,' it's 'Rose and I,' right? I mean, that's the good English way to say it."

I suppose I knew that was the actual right way to say it, but it just didn't make sense to me. I was sick and tired of not being considered. "No thanks Pop. I should go first. I'm the one talkin', and I'm talkin' about myself so I should come before Rose."

Pops burst out into the biggest belly laugh I had heard from him in a long time. He picked me up and swung me onto his back as we kept walking home together. For a split second, it was just me and Pops, but I knew that

Rose was waiting inside for us.

"I'm going to feel the way I feel and I think everyone else should, too."

Whether or not I had volunteered, I learned when we got home that I was the only one who could go with Rose anyway. The new quarry was opening the next morning, a week earlier than expected, and Pops and the boys had to make up for lost time. Unless she went on her own, I was the only one who could accompany her. The thought of her going alone, venturing out into a new life with no one by her side made me sick to my stomach. I could hardly imagine what was going on in her mind, and to tackle it alone would make it twice as hard. Because Rose is so sweet and trusting, I wanted to make sure that I was there to size up each guy she might talk to. She needed me.

My sleep came in spurts. I had dreams about men made out of shadows. We were walking down our pathway, except it was misty and in black and white, and these figures kept sneaking up behind me and Rose, scooping us up in their silent, dark shapes. I tried to warn her, to scream and scare them off, but my voice was gone. After the third nightmare, I gave up on rest, rolling over and watching her sleep instead. I watched her chest rise and fall, arms crossed over her head. I listened to her breathe, slow and deep. In a way, I felt like I was taking her pain from her. I gave her my sleep, my saturated breaths. I would do that every time if I could.

Rain started tap dancing above me, keeping me company as my mind spun and shifted. Big fat droplets that sounded like drums on our corrugated tin roof. I crawled out of bed and tiptoed to our screen door. It had been so hot lately that the cool rain created a steamy mist on the ground. All of this, the unexpected rain and the surrounding haze, made the world look surreal, like we had stepped into a painting. Like one of those moments that feels like a time you're remembering, not actually a time you're living for real. Sort of slow motion and under water. A dream where you start to wake up and never fall all the way back asleep.

The neighborhood rooster went about his morning business and, soon after, I heard the boys start stretching and sighing. I had been sitting in front of the front door since probably four in the morning, and when I turned around I wished that I could have painted what I saw. It was nothing miraculous, nothing newsworthy, but it was my favorite thing in the world. Fern's scrawny, grass-stained leg resting on Reed's back. Ash spread out like a starfish, an arm slung across Ever's neck. Pops on his side, smaller than he should be, giving the boys all the space they needed to stretch out. I watched them slowly stir awake, joining me in the day, when Rose's eyes opened and locked onto mine. She smiled at me.

Reed stepped outside to gather their clean long johns from the clothesline and the morning started as they always do. Coffee, overalls, sandwiches for lunch wrapped in kerchiefs. Pops and Rose put some of yesterday's crawdads on the burner with the last eggs we had. No one had said a word yet, which only added to the empty, awkward feeling in the room. Our home was a lot of things, but quiet wasn't one of them. Pop made a weak smile at everybody, trying to convince us, or maybe convince himself, that all would be well. Seems to me that grown-ups feel all the same things that kids do, but they stop their feelings from bubbling up for some reason. Maybe they don't want anyone else to know how they feel. I think it would be so much easier if we didn't pretend. If we just said, "I'm angry," or "I'm scared." Covering up your emotions does nothing but harm. I'm going to feel the way I feel and I think everyone else should, too.

We did all the things I knew we would have to, like fold her dresses and pack them carefully in Mama's old carpet bag. We loved that bag. Its tough exterior was covered with thin stripes in a million shades of gold, purple, and maroon. The strap had broken a long time ago, and despite us fixing it each time, it preferred to be carried from the bottom. Mama got it as a wedding present and brought it on their honeymoon to New Orleans. Pops said she was so proud of it that she wouldn't even let him carry it. What a sight that must have been. Tiny Mama with her dainty arms, barely able to fit around the bag, and giant old Pop walking next to her, empty-handed. He didn't mind one bit though, he beamed and laughed every time he told that story, remembering how honored he was to be hers.

Now, her beloved wedding gift held her first born's three dresses - classic gingham, butter yellow, and Sunday white. It carried a few hair pins, a brush, Pop's meager savings, and the smell of home. We would take turns carrying it, but it always seemed like Mama had a hand on it, too. Like it was lighter than it should have been. I had a smaller bag, a repurposed flour sack, that held my meager contributions: a couple of coins, my summertime dress, and cornbread and lard sandwiches. We stood back and studied our bags, carefully packed and buttoned up, perched on top of our straw and feather mattress. I reached out and squeezed Rose's hand. She squeezed mine back.

While everyone else ate, I took the opportunity to slip out the front door and head to the garden before we left. I laid down and used my feet to scoot all the way back, nestled between the tomatoes and the lillies. When you lay on your back under all those leaves and look up, it's like you're in a forest. You feel real small and it's even hard to find the sky through all of it. Insect wings clicked and buzzed, and the sun just barely peeked through all the foliage, creating patterns that danced around whenever the wind blew. It smelled like earth and lily blooms and tomato leaves.

"Mama," I whispered. "I think I'm doin' the right thing. I'm sorry if I'm not." Without any warning, my chest tightened and my eyes got hot and stingy again. I took a sharp inhale and bit my lip to stop it from shaking. "Will you look over us while we're out? Will you help us figure out--"

The front door banged and Reed's voice rang out, "Hey Ivy! Come on in!"

I took the biggest breath I could fit into my lungs. The scent filled my nose and I rubbed my hands over the tomato stems, hoping that Mama heard me and knew what we needed. I closed my eyes one last time when I felt something light and soft drop onto my chest. My eyelids jerked apart and I saw that the most beautiful white lily had landed right on top of my heart. Normally only the dead blossoms fall off, but this one was in its most beautiful time. A single tear dripped down the side of my cheek.

"Thank you Mama," I whispered, and tucked the bloom into the front pocket of my tattered, trusty overalls. It was time to go.

"Be careful...be smart. Just be you, ok?"

Me and Reed met between the garden and the front door. I guess everyone noticed that I was gone during breakfast and he volunteered to come out and find me.

"You gotta wear these if you're goin' into town," he insisted, throwing my old leather shoes in my direction. Miss Mavis gave them to Rose when she was my age and they had been handed down to me. I hate wearing shoes more than anything in the whole wide world, but I also didn't want to look like a street urchin. Making a good impression on this trip was important to Rose's future. I plopped down in the dirt and started pulling them on, their edges and walls feeling foreign to my skin.

"Ivy," Reed started. He sounded tired, too. Over the past few months, his voice had gotten deeper and grittier, making him sound more and more like our dad. "I trust you, you know that? I trust you with this whole...I dunno….situation, more than anyone else. Even myself."

The door moaned its painful creak again and the rest of the boys came tumbling out. I craned my neck to peer inside and saw Pop and Rose through the screen, talking. Pops held Rose's hands in his. She nodded her head intently, but her eyes were locked on her feet. A rush of responsibility hit me. The responsibility to do well by her, to help her start a new life that was worthy of her.

"Ivy, you still with me?" he prodded.

"Hm? Oh, yup." His voice pulled me back into the present.

Reed chuckled, and he looked just like Pops in that moment.

"So," he shuffled his feet in the dirt and pushed his unruly mane out of his eyes. "Well, be careful...be smart. Just be you, ok? Someone gives you a hard time, you kick 'em where the sun don't shine and run like hell."

I couldn't help but crack a grin at that one, and my smile made Reed laugh. His laugh made me laugh, and suddenly we were both cracking up, despite the atmosphere and circumstances around us.

The door opened one last time, sounding like a cranky old man, and Rose and Pops stepped out. Her creamy skin was no longer decorated with dirt and dust, but was clean and shiny, making her stormy eyes glow like the moving waters under a full moon. She had tied up her thick waves with a clean strip of flour sack and pressed her nicest dress, the pink one with white stripes. Mama's carpet bag, tucked safely under her left arm, made her look like a lost traveler. She hugged the boys and donned a brave half-smile. Even though she was dressed up and ready to leave, even though this was sort of her idea, something about her looked younger than ever. Like a little kid wearing a costume.

"Miss Ivy," Pop called me over, leaning on his knees to be at my level. His voice sounded hollow and crackly. "Rose has the map and a bit of money, ok? I'm guessin' it'll take all of today and probably the first part of tomorrow to get through New Orleans by foot, and the same time for you to get back. When you leave Rose, make sure you get whatever money there is, and use some of it to rent a room on your way home." His words were rushed and rehearsed, like he had been practicing it.

I nodded along, but my head was light and floaty again, like when you spin around too many times playing Dizzy Bat. I know he said more, but my brain was just repeating 'When you leave Rose' over and over again, like an evil echo. The thought of getting back by myself hadn't even entered my mind yet.

"And Ivy, um..." His voice trailed off and his eyes drifted down to the ground. He rubbed one hand across his head, then both hands across his face. His dark knuckles were cracked and inflamed. "I know how this sounds, but try to get as much money as you can." He looked like a kicked dog tied up to a tree.

For the first time in my life, I didn't know what to say. "I'll see ya in a few days, Pop."

"Sometimes words just seem like they don't belong."

We all walked out of the same door, but when the boys veered right towards the quarry and we turned left towards the city, our fates seemed to be sealed. The boys headed to a predictable but dangerous job where they worked until their bodies could hardly take it. The girls headed to an unpredictable and also dangerous situation. We knew that our bodies could take it and hoped that our hearts could. We were strong and we had each other.

We watched them get smaller and smaller as they got further from home. Only when we could no longer make out the five tiny silhouettes did we turn and start down the path. We both knew that it was the last time we would be on that path together. The last time we would be at home together. Maybe the last time we would see each other. And with all that weighing on us, we couldn't find anything to say to each other. Nothing. The weight of the moment pushed out any of the thoughts or words we had with us.

The rain pittered out, only a few drops here and there, giving us a temporary break from the heat of the past few days. But our air is as thick as the swamps themselves, so after only a half an hour or so we were both sweating through the backs of our clothes. I wondered why Rose even bothered to press her dress. My leather shoes pinched and choked my feet since I was so used to going barefoot. I pulled them off and shoved them into my flour sack, making a mental note to put them back on before we approached any towns.

****

The trees on our path have this uniquely beautiful shape where they all bend towards each other, bowing down like someone greeting royalty. It makes a little arch for us to walk under, a shady and cool tunnel. Every time I walk through it, I imagine a group of forest animals having a wedding or a big summer party. I could see the shortcut to Miss Mavis's house coming up on my left and I felt a sudden urge to run straight there. I wanted to hide with her until this was over. I wanted to eat cookies and dance to the fancy radio in her sitting room. I wanted to have her dry the tears that were fighting with all their might to come tumbling out of my tired eyes. My feet brushed the plants that are a little pushed down from where I sneak through. The creek behind it called to me with its familiar babbling. My feet turned to lead, heavy and hard to move, but my body willed itself to move forward. I couldn't let Rose do any of this on her own. When I looked back over my shoulder, the shortcut was long behind me.

I used my sleeve to blot away the sweat forming on my forehead, the sun now high overhead. Rose pulled out the map and used it to fan herself. After a few more bends and curves in the trail, the dust cloud attached to my ankles faded away and the soles of my feet started to feel damp. The plants were starting to change, too. The trees on either side of the pathway, usually bold oaks and maples, were thin and lanky, stretching across so that they all connected above us. Extra shade made each step cooler than before. The branches were a little bit fluffier and they had swinging tendrils, similar to the willows that surrounded our property. Wild flowers and lillies that had lined our trail so far were turning into dark ferns that smelled of rich, wet wood. It felt about 10 degrees cooler than it had only moments ago. We still hadn't said a word aloud, but I knew Rose was seeing these changes, too. I didn't expect her to be the first one to talk.

"Ivy," she announced.

"What?"

"No, look - ivy." Rose pointed to one of the trees up ahead. It was a beastly oak tree, a giant so tall I could barely see the top, and it was completely covered in ivy. Hardly a square inch of bark was visible beneath the deep, forest green leaves that wound around from top to bottom, totally overwhelming the tree. How one vine managed to take over an ancient being like that made me feel a deep respect and awe. You can never underestimate the strength of weeds. I think they are the most beautiful things in the world.

"That's Mama," I whispered.

Rose's steps slowed and the corners of her mouth edged upwards. She smiled and nodded.

"Yeah, it is," she affirmed.

We kept walking, but it was different after that. A little bit lighter.

"Ok Rose, lemme see that map. I wanna know where we're goin' and I'm in charge so lemme see it." I leaned over to snatch it from her grip, but she jerked it upwards out of my reach.

Rose let out two big laughs. "Oh you're in charge? *Ok little weed*," she mimicked in her best Pop impersonation. I glared at her sideways and she put her hands up in the air in a sign of surrender.

"Ok, so where are we now and where are we goin'?"

"I dunno - New Orleans."

"Well I know *that*, but how do we get there? This path is gonna end at some point. Lemme see it."

Rose loosened her grip, then crumpled the map into a ball, letting it fall down at her side like curtains slipping off the window. She followed after them and then her tears followed after her. In the matter of a few seconds, Rose and everything with her was a tearful pile spewed out on the ground.

I dropped down too and put an arm around her. I wanted to shush her or soothe her, tell her everything was going to be fine, but the truth was that I didn't know whether or not that was true. I didn't know what was going to happen, or what was right. So I just sat there, holding onto her but not saying anything. Sometimes words just seem like they don't belong.

"Honey, have you never been to a restaurant before?"

The sky changed from smokey blue to ripe cantaloupe, sending streaks of yellow and gold across the heavens.

"Hey," Rose nudged me, a smile spread across her face. "'Member the skunk?"

"Nooooo!" I protested, a hand instinctively covering my nose and mouth. "Why would you bring that up? I'd almost blacked that out from my memory!"

"I will absolutely never black that out," she laughed, wiping the corners of her eyes. "I think I laughed so hard that night that I peed a little bit."

You can't spend any significant time with my family without hearing The Tale of the Skunk. When I was about four or five, I was obsessed with the idea that there was buried treasure in our neck of the bayou. Miss Mavis had just given Reed a copy of *Treasure Island*, and every night he read a chapter to us before bed. Pop made giant fires outside our little cabin, and all seven of us huddled around it, eager to hear the next twist in the adventure. The dark sky and crackling embers were the ideal setting for our adventure story. Rooting for the pirates and cheering as loud as we could, Reed would have to shoosh us before he continued reading.

About a quarter of the way through that book, I got it in my head that there was buried treasure - gold and jewels - stashed away somewhere nearby. I would rush through my chores to have extra exploring time, convinced I would find it. Any free moment I had was spent scouring the bayou for pirates' booty.

On my third night of searching, I noticed a small clearing in the brush that I had never seen before. Obviously this was a sign of pirates sneaking around and checking on their loot. I crept through the makeshift pathway, heart pounding that a swashbuckling bad guy would find me, when I discovered a huge, hollowed out log. The perfect place to hide treasure! Crawling in on my hands and knees, I found something alright. I discovered that I had rudely invaded someone else's home. A mama skunk with a new litter of four pups. Pop always tells me that my curiosity has a way of getting me into trouble and it seemed as though I had proved his point. With my eyes swollen shut, nose and mouth foaming, I stumbled back home, reaching out into the darkness like a zombie. Rose said that Fern screamed so loud when he saw me that Sylvia started howling.

Pop knew you couldn't just wash the smell out, but he couldn't remember what you were supposed to use. He was searching around in the cupboard like a crazy person. Boxes and cans were flying every which way when he finally boomed "Aha! Got it! C'mon baby!" He shoved my head into the wash bin - while everybody was crowded around cracking up and hollering - and then dumped a massive can of creamed corn on my head. He rubbed it in like he was kneading bread, and I reeked like spoiled milk for weeks. It didn't even fix the skunk smell! Me and Rose were both in stitches thinking about it. So there you have it, that's The Tale of the Skunk.

"Ever said he knew it was tomato sauce the whole time but didn't want to give it away," Rose pointed out.

"I don't know if that's a fib or not, but it makes it even funnier," I giggled.

That story turned into another retelling of the green rock, which turned into another retelling of Pop-A-Doodle-Do, and so on. Sharing all those memories helped pass the time, and before we knew it the sun had crossed to the other side of the sky.

"Alright, so about three more hours 'til we hit our stoppin' point?" I asked. My stomach rumbled and we had finished our sandwiches hours ago. It got so loud that Rose even heard it over our shuffling feet and creaky carpet bag joints.

"Probably. I think we have about four more miles," Rose looked at the map again, tracing the dark lines with her thin fingers.

The trees changed even more as we continued towards the city. They were much taller and thinner than before, giving the impression of tools lined up against a shed wall. Earlier in our walk, they felt like familiar-looking townsfolk. Now they seemed more like skeptical strangers.

****

Me and Rose talked nonstop the rest of the way to our checkpoint, a little town just on the outskirts of New Orleans called Wonder Lake. We had been walking for about seven hours at that point, and our trip was transforming from a sentencing to an adventure. We had never been away from home before, and now we were almost in a brand new town, just the two of us. The sun was sinking, flirting with the top of the treeline, and my stomach flipped when I saw the first building appear in the distance. The trees' shadows stretched across the road, now laid with cobblestones, creating an intricate lattice in front of us. I took a quick pit stop to force my feet into shoes again, rolling up the bottom of my overalls so that they didn't rub against each other.

I had been to our local town hundreds of times before, but there were only three buildings there: the general store, the post office, and the church. This town was completely different. Multiple buildings, all right next to each other, lined each side of the street. Painted in different bright colors, they all seemed to have their own purpose and function. Fancy signs perched outside each of them with their names and what they did, like "Cordelia's Spirits," and "Sabine's Hemming & Tailoring." None of them were homes where people lived, they were all stores and shops and such. Standing at the end of this main drag and looking down into the rest of town, I couldn't even see where it ended. There must have been hundreds of buildings around us.

And there were lights! Everywhere! On the shops, outside restaurants, coming from gas lamps lining the cobblestone streets, any direction we looked. The streets were as bright as ever, even while the sun was going down.

My stomach flipped around and my eyes darted in every direction. A huge grin spread across my face as I took in our new surroundings. I peeked over at Rose and immediately sensed that she was as excited as me. Maybe even more. Her eyes were bigger than a baby deer's and her mouth was open wider than a new owl at feeding time.

Snuggled between two larger shops, I spotted a redwood building across the street named "Todd's." It was one of the smaller businesses, slightly bigger than our house, and it had a sign out front that advertised "Breakfast and Jambalaya - cheap and good" painted in cracked yellow letters. Its homeyness made me feel like it would be the perfect first stop.

"Let's get some food!" I squealed, breaking away from Rose and running towards the unpainted front porch.

I had heard of restaurants before, but this was my first time seeing one for myself. We walked up to the door and my insides felt like they were made of tiny crickets, all wriggling and jumping around. I didn't know what to expect, other than there was food we could buy, but that was exciting enough. We stood outside the door and looked at each other, giggling behind our hands.

"You do it," Rose urged, hiding her face behind her hands.

"No you do it," I whispered back. She shook her head and laughed as quietly as she could.

"Ok fine I'll do it!" I blurted.

I inhaled deeply, reached out, and knocked real loud, three times. We did our best to stifle our nervous laughter, but I don't think we did a very good job. If there was anyone behind that door, they definitely noticed two hysterical girls on the other side. But much to our surprise and confusion, nothing happened. Rose swallowed and transferred the carpet bag to her other arm. I knocked again and then called out, "Hello?"

Some muffled voices sounded from the other side. I tried again, "Hello! Is anyone here?"

Heavy footsteps got louder and louder as they approached the door. As if in slow motion, the screen door in front of us pulled away, revealing the biggest lady I have ever seen in my whole wide life, staring down at our now terrified faces. Her hair, a deep maroon, was even bigger than she was, its giant curls kept hostage by a massive net that stretched around it so tight I thought it might slingshot across town. She wore a huge black apron tied around a white blouse, and carried a spatula in her hand, still dripping a fragrant sauce from whatever pot she must have been stirring a moment ago.

"Honey are you knockin' on this door to come in?" she demanded, crossing her arms and staring down at us.

I cleared my throat and looked at Rose, "Um...yes?"

The big lady doubled over and cracked up so hard I thought Pops might have heard her. Great, booming 'HA's strung together with a wheezing scream. She slapped her knee, flecks from the spatula dotting her apron, and exclaimed to herself, "Knockin' on a restaurant door. Lawd, I ain't never seen that one before!" She used her apron to wipe tears from her eyes and looked at us again. "Honeys don't you know how a restaurant works? Ain't ya'll never been to one before?"

My cheeks turned a deep, hot magenta and my stomach dropped. We both shook our heads. I kept a nervous eye on Rose, who stared down at her feet. This was more humiliating than crying in front of Ms. Mavis. Even worse than Mrs. Adur insulting me. If I could have crawled into a hole and stayed there, I would have.

"Oh…" the big lady stammered and looked behind her, like she wanted to tell someone something. Then she cleared her throat, leaned forward, and beamed down at us.

"Ok honeys you come on in. My name is Miss Lucille and this here is Todd," she waved at the man in the back of the cafe, concealed by smoke rising up from the stove. "We got the finest jambalaya in the whole N'Awlins area and we'll get ya'll fixed up."

"He told us to go have some fun, us girls, ya know?"

A wave of relief washed over me. Even though she was humongous and intimidating, something about her reminded me of a mom. I smiled at Rose and she smiled back at me. "Thank you Miss Lucille," we replied, still standing on the front porch.

"Well honeys now ya'll just come on inside," she encouraged, waving her hand at the tables behind her. "Take a seat, just go ahead and pick your favorite spot." She lumbered back into the kitchen area where she and Mr. Todd started whispering to each other while they minced onions and grabbed handfuls of spices. It was hot inside, but that only added to the atmosphere. Thick waves of sweet paprika and earthy thyme drifted through the air, while currents of hot peppers lit up the inside of our nostrils. Pots bubbled away behind us, leaving golden clouds of steam lingering above them.

The restaurant had plywood walls painted a light golden yellow, but they were so covered in New Orleans art that you couldn't find an uncovered piece larger than your hand. Mardi Gras masks, fleur de lis, and bright feathers were either painted on or tacked to the walls. Seven wooden tables, each one with two chairs next to it, dotted the old wooden floor. Behind the tables sat a half wall, partly obscuring the kitchen on the other side.

For the first time since we had wandered into this new town, I opened my eyes and noticed all the other people around. I had been too focused on me and Rose to see them before. I wondered if they had heard us knocking on the door and felt a little heat rise up into my face again. Two men wearing worn, grey work suits flanked a table in the center of the room. Not fancy suits, but suits that seemed as though they might operate tractors or work on buildings. And then there was a man and a woman together looking like they might be out on a date. His wide, tan pants, held up by suspenders, paired perfectly with a crisp, white button down shirt. Shiny blacks shoes adorned his feet, and a tan fedora topped it all off. The lady was wearing a light pink dress carpeted in long tassels, head to toe. Everything was clean and pressed, and she even had high heeled shoes that matched. A silver, sequined headband stretched across her forehead. One man sat alone in the corner, sporting a vest and straw hat, reading the paper as he enjoyed his supper. We stuck out like a sore thumb with a blister on it, but nobody seemed to really notice us. They were either deep in conversation, or jambalaya.

Not wanting to miss a single second of action, we picked the table closest to the windows so we could see what was going on outside. It was dusk, a beautiful lavender transition. While the sun tucked itself into bed, still glowing gold on the horizon, the street lamps' gentle flickers took over. The cobblestone roads softened and gleamed. Shadows stretched out and looked fuzzy. Passersby continued to roam around, popping into shops or riding in carriages from one place to another, a few automobiles clunking noisily ahead. We drank in the real life picture show, elbows resting on the windowsill and chins perched in our hands. With our backs to the restaurant, we didn't even hear Miss Lucille come back to us. We both jumped when she cleared her throat, and turned to see her towering over us as we sat in our wooden slat chairs.

"Alright little missies, we got here a bowl of Todd's famous jambalaya and a basket of hush puppies. Go on, eat up!" she commanded with a grin.

My mouth dropped open and my eyes must have bugged out of my head. The amount of food on our table was what we normally split with the whole family. I couldn't believe that we got to share all of it, just the two of us! The jambalaya steamed up so much that me and Rose could hardly see each other through it. Heavy spices and sweet sausage filled our noses and throats. Next to that, a metal bowl lined with newspaper held the most beautiful hushpuppies in the history of the whole wide world. The outsides were deep golden and crunchy, but the insides were hot and soft. You could smell the sweet corn before you even bit into it. I tore the first one in half, and then shoved the next one in in one gulp.

"'Scuse me, Miss Lucille, but about how much is this gonna cost?" I asked, trying to not to spit too much while I spoke.

She squatted down between our chairs so that her eyes were even with ours, lowering her voice to what I think she thought was a whisper. "This one's on the house, honey pies," she bubbled. Her skin was like mine, a warm olivey brown, and she had freckles all over her nose and cheeks. She patted us each on the cheek, her hand covering half of my face. "But tell me, what exactly are both of ya'll doin' out here on your own, never havin' been to a restaurant before? I've ain't seen you 'round these parts. Where are you from?"

Rose took a big swallow and her eyes darted all around the room. I could tell she wouldn't be able to think of something quick. This was why I was with her, to protect her from these situations. I had to step in and fix this before it became a problem. Having someone report us was the last thing we needed.

"Oh we're from down the road," I lied, casually tearing off another half hush puppy and shoving it into my mouth. I wanted to get in as much as I could, just in case Miss Lucille decided to throw us out for fibbing.

"Down the road?" she repeated, eyebrows raised. She crossed her arms and leaned against the wall, sounding more amused than convinced.

"Mhm. Yup," I nodded vigorously. "My Pops brought us here for the very first time, but he ran into the store with our brothers. He told us to go have some fun, us girls, ya know?" Another hush puppy down.

Miss Lucille pursed her lips and smirked, "Mhm."

"And actually," I was on a roll now, "he told us that we could even get our own place tonight, so long as it's cheap! Do you know of any real cheap, real safe hostels around here Miss Lucille?"

She nodded and tapped her chin in a sort of mock thinking. "Well now I s'pose I do. For two girls who are here with their daddy and brothers, who are at the store, and who get to stay on their own tonight…" She raised an eyebrow. I knew she didn't buy my story. I stuffed my face with as much jambalaya as I could.

And then she smiled a real big, toothy smile. "The Magnolia," she answered. "Just six blocks down Market Street. Ask Miss Melly for a shared bed in a shared room. And tell her Lucille sent ya." With that, she turned on her heels back to the kitchen, cracking up again as she shook her head and muttered to herself, "...daddy and brothers at the store..."

I had a fleeting second of worry that Rose would be upset with me for lying. She hates dishonesty. But as I slowly turned my head to peek at her, all I saw was a smile full of pride and hushpuppies.

"Ok I, let's go find our bed for the night."

"When else are we gonna be here together?"

"Bye babies! You be good and have fun!" Miss Lucille called after us as we skipped down the front steps of Todd's. Stretching and rubbing our happy tummies, we waved farewell to our giant, loving benefactor. When I turned to say goodbye one last time, I swear I saw her mop tears from the corner of her eyes. My heart ached, and for a moment I wished that I could stay there forever. The kindness of strangers can be the most touching thing in the world.

The six block walk was straight through the famous French Quarter, and before we even saw anything worth noting, we could hear it. Three street performers on a standup bass, violin, and trumpet, played a bouncy tune while their fourth bandmate was on vocals. Dressed in a beige, wrinkly button down and brown slacks with matching suspenders, he sang a funny song about an obedient heart and cocktails for two. I was awestruck, frozen to the cobblestones as their notes floated around my head. When Rose came back and grabbed my arm, the singer winked at her. She may have hurried me along, but I saw her blush when we left.

As we rounded the corner, a newspaper boy the size and age of Fern carried an armful of papers, yelling "Bandit lovers Bonnie and Clyde shot to death in nearby Gibsland! Read all about it!" Men in overalls and ladies in girdles all rushed him to read the tragic and yet predictable ending of the love story that had held the nation captive. Even Solitaire was keeping up with Bonnie and Clyde. I wondered if Pops and the boys had heard the news yet. Even though I knew they were dangerous killers, something about their death made me feel sad. I wondered if they were scared at the end of it all. Rose pulled me away from the crowd forming around the newsboys and we bumped into a produce stall overflowing with okra and pecans. They taunted us with enticing smells of deep fried oil and cinnamon.

"Bag of fried okra and roasted nuts - only 10 cents for the ladies!" the vendor bellowed at us.

"Oh no thank you," Rose smiled politely.

"Oh yes please!" I countered, elbowing her in the side.

"Ivy what are you doing?" she scolded.

"Todd's was free! Let's try something new. Please?" I begged. "When else are we gonna be here together?"

And then my big sister was my hero for the thousandth time in our lives. Rolling her eyes and shaking her head, she smiled at me as she fished out a dime from the bottom of Mama's carpet bag.

"Good choice," the vendor winked as he handed us a greasy paper bag.

Munching on our hot and salty snacks, we pushed past the produce stalls and into another alleyway. The music from the first group of musicians began to transition to another troupe of buskers up ahead, all against the backdrop of people chatting, haggling, and laughing. Neither of us could help but notice a bright pink building on our right, its second floor balconies covered in hanging ferns and vines. Sweet smoke poured out of its front door as we walked by, and a small Voodoo talisman hung in the center of the first window. We shuffled along with the crowd, and when I looked over my shoulder to get another peek at the strange house, a black cat sat in the window. I gasped and tugged at Rose's sleeve, but she pointed straight ahead.

A tall, thin building caught her attention just a block in front of us. Black shutters decorated its open windows and green metal railings were adorned with roses and fleur de lis. A large white sign above the door let us know that we were at our destination. We held hands and sprinted across the street, darting between carriages and automobiles.

Tipping my head back, I emptied the remnants of our paper bag into my mouth. Too consumed by the hot, salty crumbs, I didn't realize that we had drifted inside until I felt the cool breeze of ceiling fans on my face. I tucked the empty wrapper into my overalls, unable to close my mouth.

"I didn't know places like this were real," I whispered to Rose. I could sense her nodding beside me, but I dared not turn my gaze away from what was in front of us. We had just entered through the front doors of The Magnolia Hostel.

"I'm findin' myself havin' a hard time sayin' no to you."

One hot summer night last year, all of us kids were playing stickball in the yard after dinner. Pop's voice pierced our fun as he hollered for us to get to him down by the bayou. We dropped our game and took off, thinking that he had had a run-in with a gator or Crazy David. Reed ran so fast I swear his feet didn't even touch the ground. Once we got there, all hearts pounding and scared out of our wits, we saw why Pops was yelling. It was the most magical sunset in the history of the universe. The sky was hot pink and yellow and purple, and the fireflies were darting in and out, making it sparkle. One last sunbeam pierced through the middle of it, glowing cornflower blue and hot white. We froze, so struck by what we saw that we couldn't even speak. Reed draped his arm over Rose's shoulder, who then put hers around Reed's waist. I grabbed Pop's giant hand. While the sky dazzled and danced, we stood perfectly still, wrapped up in each other and drinking in each twinkle and shadow. Walking into the Magnolia was just like that moment.

The floor wasn't just one regular floor, it was hundreds and thousands of different tiles, every color and pattern that you can imagine. Some were as yellow as sunflower petals, and others were the shade of red we saw on the edge of the sun on that special summer night. Black and white zig zags intersected with green polka dots. Stretching out in every direction, no two tiles were the same. I scanned the ground, trying my best to remember each tiny square. Mirrors covered the walls, making everything seem even larger and more grandiose. Way up above us, probably four times higher than the ceiling in our house, hung a light made up of hundreds of tiny lights, all hanging on to each other by golden threads. Not only did it brighten up the entryway, but each miniature glow reflected off of the tiles, making them twinkle and dance.

I felt like electricity was pulsing through my body, making me tingle from head to toe. I wanted to see more, to run to every end of this magical building and inspect each corner, to yell and jump and cartwheel. But I also didn't want to rush a single second of it. My steps were slow and deliberate, heel-toe, heel-toe. I wished that I could float because I didn't want to cover up any of the tiles as we walked. My eyes were glued to the rainbow mosaic floor. So much so, that I didn't see what was in front of me until the top of my head collided with something cool and hard.

"Ouch! What the heck?" I shrilled, touching a tender spot on my forehead. We were at the end of the technicolor corridor, and there sat a massive, intricately carved wooden desk. It was a beautifully deep cherry color, and I had just bashed into it. Rubbing a sore spot on the crown of my head, I noticed that it was covered in stories - angels battling and people watching on. Like a picture book of good versus evil. Maybe two inches were between my face and a scene of God talking to an angel when I heard someone clear his throat right above me.

"Aaahh!" I yelped, jumping back so far that I fell backwards, sprawled out on the floor like a terrified starfish. My eyes refocused and I looked up to see a tiny man with a tiny pencil mustache and tiny wire glasses staring down at us, an entertained yet skeptical look on his face.

"Ahem," I cleared my throat, sitting up and awkwardly brushing off my overalls. We all heard the rustle of the greasy paper bag in my pocket.

"Um, hi, Sir," I waved at him.

"Well hi to you too," the man stated, blinking a tight smile at us. "How can I help you ladies?"

"He called us ladies," I tittered out loud to Rose. The last thing you could call us in that situation was ladies. We were dirty and sweaty, wearing a tattered, ill-fitting hand-me-down and overalls with a greasy snack bag in the pockets. I was so overwhelmed and embarrassed that I couldn't help but get a mean case of the giggles. Rose shot me a stern look, but I was beyond help at that point.

"Ladies," I chuckled some more.

"Yes, um, hi," inhaled Rose, shuffling her feet. "Miss Lucille sent us to Miss Melly for a shared bed in a shared room." And while her voice was a bit shaky and she bit her bottom lip when she finished speaking, everything she said sounded correct and accurate. I nodded in support and cleared my throat, trying to get my giggling under control.

The man sat back and relaxed as he drew in a deep breath. "Ah Lucille," he fawned, leaning over and flipping through a gigantic, leatherbound book next to him. He smiled as he shook his head, like a parent remembering a funny story of their mischievous child.

"Unfortunately, Miss Melly isn't working tonight," he responded. We looked at each other in panic and my pulse quickened. Rose caught her breath. If we couldn't stay here, we would be out on the street. And while sleeping outside was old hat for us, sleeping outside in a foreign town was another situation entirely.

"But," he continued, "that's alright, because I see here that we have one open bed left." A shock of relief coursed through our bodies. "It's in our communal room," he continued. "It has ten bunk-style beds and a shared restroom. Nine and half of the bunks are taken already, so you would have to share a mattress. Technically, you will be occupants 20 and 21. It's a great group in there though, don't think they'll mind you at all." He said that last part with a wink. A group? What kind of group is made up of 19 people sharing a motel room?

Rose looked at me with a question on her face and I gave her a confident, reassuring nod as I stood back up and brushed myself off. I was so relieved to have a safe bed for the night that I didn't care who the rest of the people were. We would take care of each other.

"Since we're sharin' a mattress," I asked with a raised eyebrow, "we only pay for one person, yeah?"

His eyes narrowed and he stared right at me like he was taking aim at a target. I'm real good at staring contests, so I locked eyes right with him, putting one hand on my hip. I leaned my other elbow on his desk for a confident, nonchalante effect, only to realize that the desk was a little tall for me, so my elbow was awkwardly above my shoulder. In my head, I was tough and formidable, but I'm not so sure that I looked like that from the outside. I heard Rose stifle a laugh behind me but I had to stay in character.

"Lucille really sent you two?" he inquired.

"Yep."

He paused a long pause, then cracked a half smile. "I don't know who you two are, but I'm findin' myself havin' a hard time sayin' no to you."

I jumped up and shook the man's hand. "We'll take it!" I had never felt so powerful as when I proudly handed over the $1.80 to cover our bunk for the night.

"Ok you two," he continued. "To become genuine guests of The Magnolia you need to sign your legal names in our guest book," he said, flipping to the back pages in the massive album. It felt magical to include my names among all the other travelers and vagabonds who had been here before us. I had signed my name lots of times before, but never in any official capacity. Usually it was just in the dirt with a stick. The pen trembled in my hand, making my signature look even younger than it was. Rose took her time signing and made a pretty swirl at the end of the 'n' in Green.

"Well, let's make it official," the desk man invited. "Now that I know you are Ivy and Rose, you can call me Mr. Sebastian." He walked around from the back of the desk and stuck out his hand for both of us to shake. He was shorter than I had expected, an inch or two under Rose, but his hands were warm and his smile was much softer than it was when we first arrived. He led the way as we followed a few steps behind him, going back down the hall of beautiful tiles and up a deep brown wooden staircase that had three whole turns in it. There were ten or eleven doors on the second floor, but he left us at the first one.

"Have fun," he hinted with a wink, then turned on his heels and retreated back to his desk.

"You're too pretty not to get to pick your fella."

I waited for Rose to reach out and pry the door open, but knew that she was waiting for me to do the same. The butterflies started flitting around in my stomach again, both excited and nervous to see where we would be for the evening. Rose's delicate fingers traced the door's intricate carvings of vines and flowers, reaching and growing up towards large brass hinges. She closed her eyes and smiled, breathing in the scent of expensive wood. As bizarre was our reason for being there, I didn't want to shortchange how incredible this experience was turning out to be. We had eaten in a restaurant and were about to check into a hotel room. The two Green sisters from the swamp. If you ignored the questionable, if not twisted reason for us being here, the adventure itself was remarkable.

Me and Rose looked at each other and then back to the door. My mind raced with what might be only inches away from us. A circus troupe? Maybe their monkeys were with them! Or it could be a team of traveling bandits, working together to steal from the rich. My hopes were high that it was bandits. I always knew I would make a great thief. Maybe I could be the one who distracts the guard as everyone else loots the joint. I could be better than Bonnie and Clyde! The anticipation gave me knots in my stomach, and I couldn't take it any longer. Using both hands to turn and push, I grabbed the tarnished knob and urged it inward. It was even heavier than it looked, and I needed to use my body weight to budge the massive slab of wood. It creaked open and we got our first glimpse of what was inside.

Nothing. Empty. There wasn't a person in sight. My shoulders drooped and I tried to shake off the frown that was crawling across my face. We stood in mutual disappointment of the emptiness.

"This must be our bunk, I. There's nothin' on it." I glanced at the bed she referenced, but once I paused to examine the room, I realized that she was right about more than one thing. That lone bunk was the *only* thing in the room with nothing on it. I scanned each bed and side table, realizing that the whole place was dripping with musicians' belongings. No one was here now, but anyone could see that it had been a real showstopper earlier in the day.

The room had the same deep wooden floors as the hallway, and a row of five steel bunks lined each side wall. Small tables, sitting chairs, and dressers were dotted throughout the center of the room, as well as under the big French windows that lined the back, brick wall. The top bunk closest to us had so many strings of beads hanging down that it resembled a curtain. A shiny drape of purple, gold, green, and red. The bunk below it wasn't even visible underneath a black trombone case that hung open, lined with soft velvet the color of goldenrods. The instrument was so shiny that I could see myself in it when I leaned over. My face looked wide and fat, and I stuck my tongue out and giggled. A small table off in the corner had several empty champagne bottles and some cigarette butts. The whole room smelled like sweet wine and even sweeter cigars. I couldn't believe we got to be there. This new world had sucked me in so deeply that it seemed like the old one wasn't even there anymore. Rose was only a few feet ahead of me, running her fingers across a huge feathered headband that featured blue jewels and the feathers of a peacock. I ran down the next row of bunk beds, arms outstretched, touching silky scarves, punchy sequins, and smooth drumsticks. We squealed with delight, and I had just wrapped someone's snow white feather boa around my neck when we heard a large bang.

When the door flew open, slamming against the wall with a thunderous crash, we both yelped and froze, boa still perched around my neck. Miss Mavis once taught me the word 'cacophony.' I had been complaining to her how frustrating it was when Rose was trying to teach me how to read while all five boys (I counted Pop in the mix) were wrestling and having gladiator competitions. She nodded and sagely commented, "Yes it's difficult to focus with a cacophony of children nearby." That memory flitted into my mind when our nineteen bunkmates poured in.

A jazz band! I saw two women and a young man first, arms tangled around each other, singing a sad love song in harmony. Three men bounded in behind them, singing the same song, but in a more joyful, playful way. One of them lovingly smacked the back of the man in front of him. A few more strutted in doing the drums, cigars hanging out of the sides of their mouths. They used their hands on their legs to keep some beats, and one of them had sticks he tapped on the walls, bed frames, anything he walked past. The mix of notes was oddly captivating, an orchestra of tin, drywall, and footsteps.

"Gregory, that last note was as flat as a flapjack!" the tall, thin drummer teased, bent over double from laughing so hard at his friend.

"Oh gimme a break! You know I'm better on the ivories than I am singin,'"
Gregory responded, unoffended.

I smiled at these friends, safely spectating from behind the railing of our
bunk, huddled next to Rose and unseen by everyone around us.

A few more ladies sauntered in next, wearing black cocktail dresses and
smoking cigarettes out of long, golden cigarette holders so that they didn't
mess up their perfectly made up faces.

"So do you think I should go with Moulin Rouge or Classic Scarlet for
tonight?" one woman asked her friend, pulling out two shimmering tubes
of lipstick.

"Mmm...I'd go with Moulin Rouge. It's a little more orange and that would
look perfect with your gold dress," she responded. They collapsed into a
bunk less than ten feet from us, adding to the sound and energy that made
it almost impossible to sit still.

When it seemed like the room was about to pop, like the walls were far
beyond their capacity, he walked in. The undeniable leader of the group.
Everything around him moved in slow motion, glowy, like there was a halo
behind him. I glanced over at Rose, but she forgot that I was even there.
Her eyebrows were raised way up high and her mouth was partially open.
Her waves had pushed themselves way out of this morning's headband,
framing her stormy eyes and making her look older and more mature than
when it was pulled back.

We both stared at him while the happy chaos continued booming all around us. His dark, curly hair bounced around as he talked to one of the drummers, and a smile, or perhaps a smirk, never left his face, even when he spoke. His wide, emerald eyes were piercing against his golden brown skin, almost like they glowed in the dark. I had never in my whole wide life seen anyone like him before. Me and Rose stared at him like a pair of dumb fools, protected in our little bubble, when he looked straight at us. Locked right onto our eyes. I thought my heart was going to pop out of my chest.

"Whoah ho-ho!" he shouted, keeping his gaze on us. "My friends!" The room quieted down almost instantly, music and conversation halting like water meeting the wall of a dam.

"It seems as though we've tragically neglected to notice two newcomers to Room 115." Everyone else followed his guidance and looked at us, too. 19 people. 38 eyeballs. That was almost as much as our whole neighborhood.

"I do apologize on behalf of myself and our merry little band for not yet introducing ourselves," he drawled in a thick, dreamy New Orleans accent. He strolled through a tangled mess of legs, whispers, and cigarette smoke, then reached out his hand to shake ours.

"I'm Gilbert," he announced with a grin. "And this here is The New Year Sunrise Band." Everyone around us shouted 'hello' or 'welcome,' and I think I heard a 'bonjour,' too. Then, as quick as a snap of your fingers, all the noise resumed and everyone went back to what they had been doing a few seconds earlier. A beautiful cacophony of horns and laughter and high heels. But Gilbert didn't go back to his spot by the door. He sat down right next to us on our little bottom bunk.

"What are your names, ladies?" he inquired, seeming genuinely interested. I don't know why, but I was instantly comfortable with him. I liked him right away.

"I'm Ivy, and this here is my big sister, Rose," I announced proudly. I elbowed Rose in the side and she smiled, her eyes darting up for a second, then returning to the ground in front of her. Her shyness had overwhelmed her, but I hoped more than anything that she would sit up straight and talk to this magical man.

"Well those are lovely names," he complimented, pushing the curls out of his eyes. "Now can I ask what two such young ladies are doin' here on their own?" Even though he called us young, he seemed to be about Rose's age. Maybe a few years older, but not any more than that.

My confusion and frustration rose as I wondered why we hadn't planned a better fake story during our whole walk over here. We certainly had had the time, and yet there we were for the third time, scrambling for an explanation. For a second I thought about what we had told Miss Lucille, but something about him made me feel guilty about lying. He didn't seem like someone who needed to be impressed. He felt like us.

"Um," I started, "well it's like this…" My insides twisted up and I felt like I wasn't all the way there in the room anymore. Like my body was glued to the bed, safely covered by the enclosed bunk, but my mind was floating up above. My heart and spirit were tired, and I just wanted to be safe. Or maybe I just wanted to enjoy this. Or, maybe I only wanted to make sure Rose was alright. Whatever it was, I had hit emotional regulation capacity and my mouth started before my brain could stop it. "Our mama died and Pops can't feed us all anymore and so we have to find a husband for Rose in the next day or two."

Despite the din around us, I swear that I could hear Rose's heartbeat. Like her quick, choppy breath was living inside my eardrum. I wanted to dig a hole deeper than the Mississippi and crawl into it. I wanted the dirt to fall on top of me until I couldn't breathe anymore. Rose sat so still that she looked like a statue, like if she stayed silent enough, then maybe she wouldn't exist. Gilbert's thick eyebrows pressed towards each other, and he shook his head just a little bit. It was the first time the smile had fallen from his face.

He reached out and grabbed one of Rose's hands. "You two are comin' to our show tonight and I won't take no for an answer. You're too pretty not to get to pick your fella." Rose looked at him and blushed. She gave us both a small smile and shrugged her shoulders.

$$\text{“Well come on over, sugars.”}$$

With a wink and a nod, Gilbert stood up and walked away. Just as abruptly as he had sauntered into the bunk, he was now gone, teasing some bandmates about a solo gone wrong. I knew no one else would pay us as much attention as he did, and my heart sank a bit as I watched him rejoin his party.

"What do we do now?" Rose wondered. Even though we were only inches apart, we had to nearly yell in order to hear each other.

"Maybe we ask someone how to get to the club?" I suggested.

"Ivy, if he really wanted us to come he woulda told us how and when to get there," Rose sulked.

"If he didn't want us to come, he wouldn't have invited us!" I protested. "This is a once in a lifetime opportunity! I am not passin' by this chance to go to a jazz club in New Orleans with a tall drink of water like that." I didn't realize that I was yelling quite as loudly as I was, but two of the flapper ladies on a nearby bunk started to giggle when they heard that.

I knew that I would be more persistent about this than Rose would be, but she seemed to be considering it. She sighed and her face contorted for a minute, like she was solving a math problem without pencil and paper. I could tell that she was weighing the pros and cons, always so careful about each decision she made. After a few seconds, she pursed her lips, straightened her shoulders, and turned square towards me.

"Ok," she relented.

"Really?" I squealed, grabbing her by the elbows.

"Yeah, let's go." She smiled at me and nudged my leg with hers. Shock and joy pulsed through me that she had agreed to such a spontaneous adventure.

"Hallelujah!" I jumped up and screamed. The same flappers that had giggled at us just a second ago now whispered to each other behind their hands. One of them nodded to her friend, whose eyebrows rose up, clearly intrigued by whatever her pal had just shared. My heart pounded as I watched them walk over to us, fight or flight starting to kick in.

"Rose and Ivy, right?" She was tall and thin and elegant and perfect. Her lips were bright red and she had hoop earrings the color of a corn field. A black, fringed dress framed her body, and her mocha hair was set into beautiful pin curls, secured with a beaded headband. I wondered if she was a movie star.

"Yeah, that's right," I confirmed, standing up and trying to look tall.

The beautiful lady smiled. "How 'bout a little makeover before the show?"

My heart felt like it had just run all the way to Miss Mavis's. Me and Rose looked at each other and grinned, but the pretty lady was already unzipping a bag of makeup on the next bunk. Her friend motioned to us.

"Well come on over, sugars."

"I look beautiful."

Bobbette and Mary Jane, but Bobbette liked to go by Bobbie and Mary Jane liked to go by MJ. While the band tuned strings, polished brass, and packed up their instruments, MJ and Bobbie tuned our locks, polished our skin, and unpacked their makeup bags. Never in my whole wide life had I worn makeup, and my hair was as overgrown as my name. But, with some love and attention from the girls, my crown was so shiny and powerful that anyone around me could see it as much as I could feel it. Queens helping queens.

The whole time they brushed, curled, and rolled our hair, they told us about their adventures on the road. They were from a small town on the other side of New Orleans and had known Gilbert since before they were my age. In fact, they had grown up just a few houses away from each other, and Bobbie's grandma taught all three of them in Sunday School classes.

"We loved Sunday services and all," MJ mused as she set Rose's hair into pin curls, "but music was always the most important thing to all three of us, wouldn't you say, B?"

"Oh no doubt about that," Bobbie answered, puckering her lips at me to demonstrate blending my new lipstick. "After school or church, we would run over to our house and copy whatever we heard on the radio, singing, dancing, and playing all kinds of instruments together."

"You play instruments, too?" I gasped. What couldn't they do?

MJ giggled as she blended some coal black pencil into Rose's lash line. "We do! Gee between the two of us we must play five or six instruments."

"Still not as many as Gilbert, though," Bobbie responded, MJ nodding in agreement.

"So you can see how we got here," MJ continued. "When he turned 17, Gilbert quit school and decided to start a jazz band. In the last two years, we've built up our group and toured all around The South, making this a full time job. It was Gilbert who personally recruited each and every soul here in Room 115."

"He's always been passionate and charming, that one," mused Bobbie with a smile. "So when he said they'd need singers and dancers, we were the first to sign up."

"A lot of people think all three of us are siblings since we're so close like that. Like sisters and brother," MJ added.

"Are you two sisters?" I asked.

"Cousins actually," Bobbie responded. "But my mama passed when I was real tiny, so my auntie raised me alongside MJ."

"We're sisters," MJ added with a wink.

I looked at Rose in shock but she hadn't heard, too distracted by watching Gilbert and Gregory tinker with a new song at the piano in the center of the room. But this was too big of a coincidence to ignore.

"Our mama died too!" I blurted out. "She died birthin' me, but it wasn't my fault."

Bobbie gasped and MJ took my hands. "No baby," she exclaimed. "No it was absolutely not your fault, and -" she took one of Rose's hands as well. "She must've been a wonderful woman to have made you two. I know she's proud." We both blushed a little bit, but my happiness far outweighed any embarrassment. While I expected Rose to nudge me or shoot me a look, she actually leaned back and smiled. It was nice having someone else understand what we had gone through. After a lifetime surrounded by our beloved boys, we were in seventh heaven getting to be in the company of other girls.

"Now," Bobbie boomed in a theatrical voice, "for your big reveal!" She pulled out a beautiful bronze mirror with golden Forget-Me-Nots engraved all over the back of it, then turned it around so we could see ourselves.

I breathed in so much air so fast that I choked, and MJ threw her head back and laughed. There was no way that the person in the mirror was my reflection. I looked like a real girl, like *my* name could have been Rose. My hair was clean and shiny, and my curls wiggled when I shook my head. My face glowed and my smile was so big that even my eyes beamed.

But the real Rose? She looked like an actual woman. Her eyes, shaded and outlined, highlighted their beautiful almond shape. Her lips were red and shiny, making her teeth seem even whiter. Deep golden waves framed her small nose and rosy cheeks. Anyone on the street would have thought that she was a singer up on stage with Gilbert and the rest of the band. Miss

Mavis had a portrait of her daughter in one of her hallways, and I always thought she was the prettiest woman I had ever seen. Rose looked just like her.

"Wow," whispered Rose, gently touching her cheekbone as though to check that she was real. "I look beautiful."

"You *are* beautiful," Bobbie corrected her, squeezing her shoulder.

She looked down at the familiar pink dress I saw her wear so often, dull, ill-fitting, and frayed. She tugged at the hem, trying to smooth out the front. Even with the neck-up makeover, our clothes made it clear that we were bayou folk. You just can't compare overalls to a cocktail dress.

"Do you...do you have a dress that I could possibly borrow?" Rose asked, sheepishly.

Both dancers sprang into action, digging in their trunks for something Rose could wear. Shawls and scarves flew every which way, leaping through the air and landing on whatever suited them. A silky black jacket landed on my head as they argued over which piece would be best for her. Finally, they agreed on something. While MJ held up a blanket as a fitting room, Bobbie tied and zipped and pinned Rose into the most elegant midnight blue dress. Covered in silver beads and pearly gems, it traced her figure perfectly, starting with off-the-shoulder straps and ending at her knees. MJ had the same size foot and they dug out some black heels to go with. Rose had worn Mama's only pair of heels a few times before, and she somehow took to them naturally, strutting from bunk to bunk.

They tried to find something for me too, but I was too small. Instead, they put Rose's pink dress on me and pinned it up to fit. MJ wrapped my shoulders in a gold shawl with sequins sewn all over it, and then Bobbie covered my neck in so many beaded necklaces that I was afraid I would tip over. A maroon hair band with a feather on the side went across my forehead and framed my face just so. I may not have looked as sophisticated as the other girls, but there was no doubt that no one else would have my look. We were real life Cinderellas, with *two* fairy godmothers, no mice, and a jazz band!

Bobbie made me do a twirl to put my whole outfit on display, and she clapped and whistled as I hammed it up, curtsying and waving at a pretend audience. MJ was putting on fresh lipstick for herself when we heard Gilbert's voice cut through the noise.

"Ok gang, let's hit it!" He vanished from the room even quicker than he had arrived.

"You better slow down or you might take my place!"

"I don't understand," Bobbie pondered, shaking her head. The four of us sat on two bunks across from each other, leaning forward so that our knees almost touched. "Everyone knows how to dance, you just gotta feel the music!"

With most of the band away at sound check, we had more space to practice what I had learned would be the most important lesson of the evening. Dancing.

"Even if I feel the music, I won't know what to do," Rose admitted, chewing on her lower lip. "I just can't dance."

The girls stared at each other and looked as though they had been tasked with an unsolvable crisis.

"Well we don't believe in any of that," MJ reassured with a dismissive wave of her hand. "Anyone can dance if they just start movin'. Stand up."

Rose looked at me and I shrugged my shoulders.

"Stand up!" MJ exclaimed as she led the way. "We'll teach you our favorite dance right now. It's called the Charleston and absolutely anyone can do it."

Bobbie bounced over to a record player in the corner of the room, her bare feet taking a break from the fancy heels, and shuffled through a pile of records. She placed one on the player and moved the arm until we heard a loud scratch, followed by an explosive trombone entrance. A piano tumbled in after it, making the tune so jumpy and joyful you couldn't help but tap your toes. MJ hummed and moved her body in such a way that I could hardly tell how she was doing it. It looked like her limbs were disconnected, maybe broken, but she somehow managed to look amazing while doing it. We had lots of practice dancing around the fire, but it never looked like that.

"Ok dolls, your turn. Just pull your feet in and out like this, and then swing your arms like this," she demonstrated.

I felt like a crooked bird trying to take flight, but I didn't even care. With each swing of my arms, I got bigger and bolder, like a loopy dodo just happy to be alive.

"Well now I don't know about that bein' The Charleston," MJ puzzled, "but it's somethin'!" She and Bobbie cracked up, but cheered me on nevertheless.

"It's not The Charleston," I shouted over the trumpet solo. "It's my own dance. It's The Bayou!" As my body swung in all sorts of directions, I couldn't help but think of the turtles that would awkwardly scoot through the muck of the swampy shores.

The song ended and I collapsed back onto our bunk, panting and heaving and laughing. A followup song started and I looked up just in time to see Rose in all her glory. If I had been a muddy turtle then she was a soaring egret; long, thin, strong. Her arms and legs were moving just like MJ. They only showed her how to do it once, but she took to it as though she had been doing it for years. If I had magically appeared in that room, if I hadn't witnessed the transformation with my own eyes, I could have walked right by her and not even recognized her as my own flesh and blood.

"Hey girl, you might just find yourself walkin' outta here with a job," Bobbie teased. "You better slow down or you might take my place!"

"Ok, phase two of your jazz life makeover is complete," MJ announced, catching her breath. "Outfit? Check. Charleston? Check. Now you gotta learn to -" she said this next part in a pretty, trilly voice. "- Siiiiiing!"

The girls sang along with the next record, harmonizing the main part, and they sounded like one person with two different voices. It was the prettiest thing I had ever heard in my whole wide life. Pops and Rose had been singing together every evening since she could talk, so I knew she would be amazing at this part.

"Ok baby, try this note," Bobbie cajoled. "It don't mean thing if it ain't got that swiiiiiiing."

Rose jumped right in and sounded so beautifully natural that it made it seem as though they had always been a trio instead of a duo.

"That was real good!" MJ proclaimed, making Rose blush slightly. "Now go a little higher on that last note. See, I'm at a G there. You stay right here at E…" While I listened in silent support, I decided at that point that my talents were more in percussion.

"Alright gang," MJ declared as she put out a cigarette and threw on a red tasseled shawl. "It's showtime."

"C'mon baby girl, let's go!"

"Do it," Bobbie whispered in my ear.

My hands were wrapped around the top of the banister, just at the beginning of a thought of sliding down the two story staircase. I grinned at the twinkle in her eye, threw one leg over the other side, and let go.

Rose and MJ were halfway down the stairs when I whizzed by them, waving and giggling, a giddy blur of beads and feathers gliding down the railing.

"Ivy Jean!" Rose half-scolded, but I could tell she was far from upset about it.

"Goodbye ladies, have a pleasant evening!" Mr. Sebastian called to us.

"Ta-ta, Basty! Don't wait up!" MJ teased as we bounded across the magical tiles, bursting into the warm night air.

My little legs worked as hard as they could, but I still trailed a few steps behind. When I barged out of the door, I slammed right into Rose's back, not realizing that they had stopped.

"You ok?" I huffed.

"I'm fine, I'm fine, I just -" she paused, inhaling deeply. I admired the beauty of my big sister, night lights reflecting in her shiny, hopeful eyes. "I can't believe we're here! Look!"

The same blocks we had walked only a few hours earlier had transformed into the most extraordinary place my imagination could ever conjure up. Gas lamps dotted the cobblestone street, dancing and flickering and tricking the nighttime into thinking it was awake. The buildings lining each side of the street were so close together that they stood shoulder-to-shoulder, like joyful soldiers at attention. Each one was painted in its own style - royal purple, forest green, sunshine yellow. Even though it was dark out, everything somehow seemed more colorful, more bold, than it had during the day.

Each playful building's balcony overflowed with people singing and dancing. Every doorway we passed oozed its own music, snares and trumpets and clarinets, but somehow nothing clashed. Like each song let its neighbors occupy their own space. No matter where you looked, even if you closed your eyes, the beat ran right through you. A rhythm pulsing through the city itself. It was a magical place that drew its power from music.

Rose and I strolled hand-in-hand behind MJ and Bobbie, but I ached to break away and go into one of the music halls. Each doorway we passed gave me a peek into another venue. One poured out ragtime piano, the next one a deep string bass, and then the telltale sound of good jazz - the trombone.

Just when it was almost too much to resist, when I was about to make a break for it and dive into a club across the street that was playing some scat, I turned my head at just the right time to see "Economy Hall" on the large brick building we were about to enter. Outside the front door lounged six men in deep gold and maroon suits and fedoras, smoking cigars and laughing together. They whistled and winked at our group, and I laughed out loud when Bobbie and MJ just walked right by. They pretended they didn't even see those guys as they swaggered into the jazz club, flaunting their own crowns.

When we walked through the front door, everything changed forever. It was like nothing I had ever seen, heard, or even imagined before, and I never wanted to leave. The second the doors cracked open, it was like the music turned into water and flooded over our whole bodies. Like it was soaking into me and I could swim in it if I tried. It washed over my skin and saturated my hair. It splashed the floor and absorbed through my feet, traveling all the way up to my head. I closed my eyes and took a deep breath, trying to breathe in the bass, trombone, and snare drum. I wanted to drown in it. Tears flooded my eyelids even though I wasn't sad. I was the opposite of sad. I was so overwhelmed by joy that my body couldn't hold it in on its own. That music drenched every single part of me, body and soul. Someone's hand on my shoulder brought me back to Earth. "You gotta move, doll," a strange man urged. I was so taken by the moment that I had stopped dead in my tracks in the doorway, holding up the line. "Sorry, pal!" I shouted, and pushed myself forward to find Rose again.

It was dark inside, but my eyes adjusted after standing there for a minute. The room was full of rich cherry wood tables and chairs, with soft, velvety crimson couches lining the sides of the hall. Every single seat was filled up by beautiful people, men and women, and some seats even had two people in them. In any direction I looked, I saw legs and feathers and cigarette holders. This amazing tangle of bodies all centered around a dance floor in the middle of the room. It seemed impossible that they could move, let alone dance, since there were so many people occupying the floor. And some of them were doing the Charleston! It smelled like cheap, sugary cigar smoke and the bourbon Pops has a glass of on Christmas.

Despite the distractions and marvels that surrounded me in every direction, none of it was a match for the stage, the clear centerpiece of the hall. Raised above the ground so that everyone could see, there was no confusion about what was most important here. Music. There must have been twenty people on stage. Trombones, trumpets, drums, a standup bass, singers, you name it. Yet again I felt my feet cement themselves to the stained walnut floor; I couldn't help but stand still and drink in every last detail. I had no idea how far ahead my group had gone.

"C'mon baby girl, let's go!" Bobbie appeared behind a couple at the bar and grabbed my hand, pulling me through the crowd. I must have been following along, but it felt like my feet had lifted off and my body was simply floating by, being pulled by my fairy godmother. We flew by high heeled feet, strings of pearls, and clean new spats until we got to a circular table right up front, big enough to fit half the band. Rose had just perched herself front and center, eyes glowing and ready to enjoy the show. One of the waiters, dressed in black slacks, a pressed white shirt, and a bowtie, winked at MJ and took away the little sign on the table that simply stated, *For Gilbert.*

"You're lookin' prettier than ever, Miss Mary Jane," the server quipped. MJ smiled and shrugged her shoulders. She opened her mouth to say something, but all at once everyone in the hall started yelling at the top of their lungs.

"They're waitin' for you."

"Oh MJ, run!" Bobbie panicked. "Girls you stay right here."

We had lost track of time. The whole hall was screaming wild because the first band had cleared the stage, and Gilbert and The New Year Sunrise Band just appeared behind the midnight blue velvet curtain. They looked extraordinary. Larger than life. Gilbert wore a navy suit with a cream fedora, and, no surprise, was smiling at each and every person in the room. I think everyone thought he was looking right at them.

Bobbie and MJ sprinted forward and made it up to the stage just as we heard him start the set. "Ladies and gentlemen," he boasted. "I have never been so excited to perform in front of such a gorgeous crowd." Gilbert was just the same to that whole big group as he was to us. Everybody whooped and whistled, and me and Rose giggled at each other.

The server who had removed the *For Gilbert* sign reappeared, holding two delicate, etched glasses with a strange, brown, bubbly liquid in each of them.

"What the heck is this?" I asked, wrinkling my nose. He threw his head back and laughed the way Pops does when he pretends to be Santa Claus.

"Baby are you serious?" he asked. "Oh honey you're in for a treat. Take a sip." Once again, my curiosity overpowered my suspicion. I gave him the side eye as I picked up my drink, inspecting the strange potion with caution.

Rose picked up her glass, too, and we each took a teeny tiny sip. It was the best thing I had ever tasted in my whole wide life. It was sweet, but also had some spiciness to it. The bubbles tickled my mouth all the way down to my throat and up to my nose.

"Mother Mary!" I exclaimed. "Is there more of this stuff?" I asked our server, eagerly gulping it down. He gave his two big 'ha's again and then answered, "I knew you'd like it. I'm Mr. Bubba, just let me know what else I can get you. Gil told me to give you ladies whatever you want."

"What's it called?" I shouted above the music, stifling a burp and pointing to my drink.

"Coca-Cola!" Mr. Bubba replied. "I'll keep 'em comin!"

The night had just started, but between the band's performance, our makeover, Gilbert's smile, and our little glasses of happiness, I could have died right there and gone up to see Mama. Our hips wiggled in our seats to the beat of the drums while our shoulders shimmied in tandem with the horns. Rose sang along while I pretended to. Rather than actually singing, I preferred to use two forks on the table as drumsticks. Somehow, in some impossible reality, we were front and center at the finest jazz club in New Orleans.

"Ladies and gentlemen," the first song had just finished and Gilbert was talking to the audience. "We have never played for such a beautiful, talented, and enthusiastic group before. And yes, I say that to everyone." The crowd cracked up. They loved him, and I understood why.

"But I have a real big favor to ask each of you," he said quietly. The hall settled down a bit, taking a cue from its leader. "The band and I have two special guests with us tonight. Two very special, never-before-seen friends of our merry little group, and it would just make my evenin' to have them up here with us." My heart pounded so hard that I swear you could have seen it through my chest.

"Would you fine, good-lookin' folks help me welcome these lovely ladies to the stage?" The crowd roared in response, and Rose's mouth literally dropped open. I immediately shot up to my feet as though I had been electrocuted, but she was frozen solid like a statue. I grabbed her arm and started pulling.

"C'mon Rose! Wake up! We're goin' up there!" She was a sack of gravel, stunned into silence. I put one foot up on the seat to try and pry her off of it. "Come on dammit!" I yelled, yanking even harder.

A steady hand on my shoulder jolted me. "Your approach doesn't seem too effective, Miss Ivy." Gilbert had come off the stage and was smiling down at us. A huge light beamed down on our table, illuminating our faces, while everyone around us whistled and clapped.

"Come along, pretty little Rose. They're waitin' for you," he encouraged, putting his hand out for her to grab. Rose looked up at him and got right to her feet, no fussing or fighting.

"Oh go figure!" I yelled at her as she smoothed down the front of her dress.

Lights and faces blurred past us as we ran up to the stage. Rose was in the middle, her left hand in Gilbert's and her right in mine. Everything around us seemed to be going fast and slow all at once, and I loved every second of it. It was crazy and impossible and we were laughing for no real reason. Two girls from the bayou, dressed to the nines and about to get up on stage with a bonafide jazz band and a real life Prince Charming. I ran ahead and got there first, but the stage was taller up close than it had been at our table. Bobbie grabbed one of my arms and MJ took the other as I kicked my legs. They hoisted me up while the crowd giggled and awed. Gilbert hopped up on his own, then reached out his arms to help Rose.

"Alright you fine folks, thanks for waitin' for these two gems," he announced back into the mic, tucking his curls back underneath his hat. The audience boiled over and Rose covered her mouth because she was smiling so big. "Hit it, Drew."

The drums started with a tat-ta-tat, tat-ta-tat, then Bobbie and MJ's voices floated over our shoulders. They sounded like angels, and when Gilbert came in it somehow got even better. Each time he picked up the trumpet, we jumped and bounced and clapped like fools, and everybody cheered even louder.

In between the choruses, Bobbie came up behind us and shouted, "'Member that move we taught you? Now's the time!" I could hardly do it the first time in Room 115, but I didn't care. I busted out The Bayou while Rose effortlessly joined the girls to dance in sync. My arms swung higher than the heavens, and my feet flew every which way. There was so much hollering and whistling that I thought the ceiling might just crumble.

If that number had been a match, then our next one was a bonfire. It was more of a swingy jazz tune, and not a single body in the hall could help but dance. Even the waiters and waitresses danced between their tables, using their serving trays as partners. The dance floor came alive as everyone pulsed together to the drums and horns. Me and Rose stood in awe as the crowd parted to let one couple in the middle have the floor. In between all their kicks and swings, they did moves I didn't even think were possible! He flipped her over his head and swung her around his back. Rose leaned over and laughed as she pushed my chin up to close my mouth. "I want to do that!" I pointed and yelled.

After that number and its thunderous applause, we skipped back to our table to find that Mr. Bubba had left us fresh plates of hot and salty fried crawfish tails, followed by sticky bread pudding. We stuffed our faces and guzzled Coca-Cola as though we had a quota to meet. Every time Gilbert opened his mouth or blew that trumpet, we whooped louder than the band's next loudest fan.

When they started playing Louis Armstrong I felt like I was going to explode. I pushed our plates aside and climbed up on top of the table, my own little stage. Rose clapped and sang along, never once telling me to get down.

Drenched in sweat, we defined joy. Bliss incarnate. I wanted to drink in every single piece of those moments. It was the best night of my whole wide life.

"You are exactly the way you're supposed to be."

"Iiiiiiivvvyyyy," I heard through a thick fog, like a voice underwater. I willed myself to pay attention, but my body was like lead and my eyes were glued shut.

"Go away Pops, it's too early," I mumbled, swatting at the air. Someone giggled at me.

"Ivy, you gotta wake up, honey. It's time for us to go."

Reality hit me quickly as everything came into focus and I remembered where we were. I shot up in my bunk and felt the headband and necklace still in place from last night. Soft feathers and smooth pearls.

"Sorry Rose, I didn't know I was out that hard. I didn't even-" I gasped. It wasn't Rose waking me up. Rose wasn't even there. Our raucous, joyful, magical Room 115 was empty. Bunks cleared and trash cans full. The band was gone.

"Honey," Bobbie started as she sat on the edge of my bunk. "We wanted to say a proper goodbye before we left town."

MJ leaned over and wrapped me up in her arms. "You two, without the shadow of a doubt, have been the best part of our stay in New Orleans." Everything had been so enchanting, so fairy tale-like, that I hadn't thought about it ending. I bit my lip hard to stop it from shaking and both girls hugged me. My heart was broken.

"Here," I sniffled, sliding off the necklace. "I still have some of your stuff."

Bobbie put her hands on my head and stopped me before I could get the headband off. "That's all yours now, baby. You wear that whenever you want to and think of us. Even if it's just cleanin' around the house." They smiled at each other and MJ cleared her throat.

"Thank you," was all I could muster. My breath was shallow and my eyes were locked on my feet, afraid that if I looked at my new friends I wouldn't be able to stop the tears from launching down my face.

"Wait," I wondered. "Where did Rose go? You gotta say goodbye to her, too!" A shot of panic ripped through me. She would be devastated if she had simply run to the bathroom and missed seeing them go.

MJ nodded towards the door. "She's in the hall, sayin' goodbye to someone else."

With shaky legs, I stood up and took a few steps towards the partially open door, cracked open just enough for me to see the right side of Gilbert's back. His voice came into focus. "...and don't go with anyone who makes you feel uncomfortable. You don't have to explain yourself or justify anything, just listen to yourself, ok?"

"Mhm. I know that now." That was Rose. Some paper crinkled and I could hear her shift her weight from one foot to the other.

"Here's our schedule for the next couple months in case you need us, or maybe you could even come visit. We're makin' our way up the Mississippi, headin' up to Chicago." It was quiet for a few breaths, but I could see Rose wrap her arms around him.

"Be smart, ok?" He continued, talking into her shoulder. "And don't be ashamed about that or anything else about you. You're exactly the way you're supposed to be. Whoever winds up with you is one hell of a lucky guy."

I had inched closer and closer to the door and saw Gibert pull away from Rose, holding her chin in his hand. Like he really cared. My throat was tight and swollen, and in that moment I wanted to both stay forever, and rush straight home. I couldn't will myself to pull away until the floorboards creaked beneath me. He spun around, looking me straight in the eyes.

"Well Sleepin' Beauty has finally woken! C'mere you magnificent creature," Gil exclaimed as he pushed the door open. "Rose can fill you in on any details, but it's time for us to start headin' to Chicago. Just booked a one-of-a-kind gig in two weeks." He held me by my shoulders so that I had to look at him. "You are just like you said your mama is. You are exactly the way you should be. You keep bein' you, Miss Ivy. And Miss Rose. The very best garden I've ever known." He gave her hand one more squeeze and smiled that smile. Although it seemed, for the first time, that it may have been hard for him to do so. He gave us a wink and sauntered down the stairs to the lobby.

I looked to Rose, who hadn't turned to watch him go. She stood in the same place she had been in when they hugged, still facing the door to Room 115.

"Well then," she cleared her throat. "I s'pose we should pack up."

And just like that, I was back in my overalls. Rose's sequined dress fell to the floor as the familiar, tattered cotton frock slowly rose back up into its place. The Cinderella story was over and our real journey stared us down. It was time to find Rose a husband.

"So it'll be like home?"

Mr. Sebastian was perched again at his wooden desk, and even though our interactions were brief, I didn't want to say goodbye. When we first set eyes on him we were anxious, expectant, even excited. But all of that had been sobered up as we faced a cold, hard reality.

"So how was it?" he smirked at us, leaning on his elbow like a friend searching for gossip. "Quite a group, that Gilbert and company, aren't they?"

"Yeah," I muscled a polite smile.

"You could say that again," Rose choked.

"Well I hope you come visit us again," he proclaimed. "You'll always have a spot available at The Magnolia."

"Thank you, Mr. Sebastian."

The hotel was a dream bubble. Like everything inside it wasn't part of real life, but something special that no one would ever know about besides us. To leave that space was to wake up from that dream and walk straight into a nightmare. We stood shoulder-to-shoulder in the entryway. Rose looked at me with a question mark on her face and I knew my job was to help her be strong. I remembered my crown, forced my chin higher in the air and gave her a confident nod. We placed our hands on the shiny brass bar and pushed the door open together.

I figured that the town we were looking for was about a three hour walk from New Orleans, but we were walking slowly. We passed by Todd's and I could almost taste the jambalaya and feel Miss Lucille's warm, gigantic body squeezing us goodbye. We walked by Union Station and could sense the vibrations of people coming and going, off to some new adventure. But as our steps increased, the buildings and people and action started to decrease. The cobblestone faded again to dirt. We had come into New Orleans on one side and went straight through out the other.

"Why did Pops pick this town?" I asked Rose. I had been so focused on the mission that I hadn't had the time to wonder that until now.

"We have some distant family friends from here," Rose started. "You know we don't have anyone besides the seven of us, so that says a lot right there. It's safe and I should be able to find a good community. Plus, it's a mining town like ours and they just hit a big find, so everyone's in good shape, financially. Most of the guys suddenly have a lot more money, so they want wives and families now."

I shifted my flour sack, balancing on one side and then the other, sweat sliding down my back. "So it'll be like home?" I asked. "Ya know, like it'll feel like home for you?"

"Yeah, I'll get used to it right away."

Two squirrels playing tag darted across our path, scurrying this way and that. "Plus," she continued, "if it all works out you guys could maybe stay with us eventually. Work in the new mine long enough to build up some savings and get a new house."

More dust and shuffling feet. The path was dry, but the trees and foliage around us were green and wet. I couldn't believe how different the world looked only a day or two ago.

Hunger poked at me again, which meant that breakfast had been a while ago. I knew we must be getting close, but I didn't want to be. As the pathway bent around a small creek with a wooden bridge, I noticed Rose stand up a little straighter.

"Look," she pointed. "I see a house."

"Anyone who spends just a minute with you is better for it."

A small valley just beyond our pathway sat nestled between a forest of oaks and a deep, babbling brook. A few rows of shanties lined the side closest to the trees, and the telltale signs of a mining town were immediately apparent to us - pump wells and soot. On the far side of the village, the opposite side of the shanties, stood a few dozen real houses. They were closest to the stream and were clearly new, fresh paint and newly potted flowers. They weren't mansions, but they were huge by our standards. They had shingles and foundations and porches and yards and gardens. Next to that were a bunch more houses in the early stages of being built. It looked like a picture I saw once on a postcard in the General Store.

"Hey," I smiled, pausing to observe the picturesque hills. "Hey Rose, this looks like home, but better! This looks real nice." Relief coursed through my tired body. I sat down under the shade of a nearby willow to have some water and take it all in. All I wanted was for Rose to be safe and happy, and it looked like that might just happen.

"You know, you could plant another garden here. Grow more tomatoes and even some rose bushes!" I mused, peering down at a particularly cute cottage with a white picket fence.

"What do you think, Rose?" She hadn't answered me once since we got to this turn in the path. "Rose?" I looked over my shoulder and saw her sitting off to the side between two saplings. Her arms hugged her knees, which were drawn up to her chest, and she gently rocked herself. I brushed off my overalls and grabbed the canteen, then walked over and settled in next to her.

"Whatcha thinkin'?" I whispered, handing her some water and putting my arm around her.

"I'm so nervous," she confided, her head tucked between her knees. Her breath was quick and shallow. "It's all come down to this." She looked up at me, tears tumbling down her cheeks. "What if no one wants me?" The sun was high overhead and cast a hot, heavy curtain all around us. Her lack of self esteem filled me with an urgent need to fix it. How on Earth could she feel that way? All I saw when I looked at her was perfection. Everyone wanted to be around her, especially me.

"Rose Diana Green," I barked. "You just performed on stage at Economy Hall. You are the best dancer, singer, cook, teacher, friend...everything! You are the best at everything!" I counted all these attributes on my fingers, pacing in front of her like a pastor on Sunday morning.

"Anyone who spends just a minute with you is better for it," I yelled. "You are magic. You are a queen. We will find someone who thinks of you just like that," I finished, wagging my finger and stomping my foot.

I had failed in stopping her tears. They fell hard and fast into the dry dirt now, but she smiled behind them. I reached into Mama's carpet bag and found a handkerchief for her. Wiping her eyes and blowing her nose, she nodded and took a deep, full breath.

"Honestly Ivy, I don't know what I'd do without you."

We walked in silence down the hill to the town. It was a beautiful walk, surrounded by wildflowers and the gentle knock of woodpeckers. My imagination took over, starting to daydream about how much she might fall in love with this new pathway. I saw her peacefully strolling down, picking a bouquet and singing her favorite songs.

"You'll do most the talkin', right?" she asked. "Because I don't think I can just yet. Soon, but not yet."

"Absolutely," I answered.

"Ok. Well then let's do this," she announced as she marched down the first driveway.

"Who do you think you are?"

The front door was made from sturdy pine and it shone in the afternoon sun, the heat making it smell like a fresh Christmas tree. My heart banged around in my chest, impersonating the little drummer boy. Rose reached out with her slim, toned arm and knocked. Three strong, sturdy knocks. Where only a few moments ago she had been uncertain and frightened, she now seemed resolved and determined. Fierce, even. We heard some metal dishes clank around and a drawer slam shut.

"Hang on!" A deep voice boomed from inside. Heavy work boots scuffed across a creaky plywood floor and panic caught hold of my breath. I glanced over at Rose, whose face was pale with dread. What would we do if this person was clearly wrong? What if he was stinky or dirty? What if he was 70 years old? I hadn't brainstormed a backup plan, an escape route, and now it seemed clear that we needed one. So I did the only thing I could think of.

"Run!" I whispered to Rose.

"What?" she gasped, wide-eyed.

"Run!" I shouted, and took off running as fast as my little legs could go. Dirt clouds pushed up around us in every direction as we neared the end of his driveway. I could hear Rose right behind me, so I didn't even dare turn around.

"Hey!" I heard the deep, gruffy voice call out. "Hey! Who do you think you are? You can't just bother a man and then run away!" But his voice faded into the dust as we ran around a bend and further down the main hill.

We ducked behind some mulberry bushes off of the path, legs burning and sweat beading around our foreheads. Our lungs worked as hard as they could, and not just because we had been running, but because we were both hysterical with laughter.

"I can't believe we just did that," Rose gasped, a huge grin splattered across her face. "Did you hear how cranky he sounded?" She sprawled out flat beneath the berry-covered leaves, chest heaving and panting.

"I think he might've been a hundred years old!" I joked between gasps.

Rose grabbed a handful of berries and sat up to enjoy their sweet tartness.

"Ok," I thought out loud, starting to catch my breath. "What if we keep doin' that?"

"Doin' what? Runnin' away?" Rose wondered, tossing a berry into the air and catching it in her mouth.

"Well, yeah," I suggested, the idea starting to solidify. "Let's knock and see what we hear. If we don't like it, we can just run away! We're faster than anyone out here."

Rose smiled and shook her head. "You are crazy and I'm so glad you're here."

****

We spent the next hour or so playing our new game, 'Knock, knock, run around the block.' The name was Rose's idea. After we recovered our breath, stretched our legs, and left the protection of the mulberry bush, we sauntered back into the main area of houses.

"Hm…" Rose pondered, evaluating the homes that stretched out in all directions around us. "Let's give this one a shot."

A sweet, unassuming yellow cottage stared us down. Marching up the porch, we knocked and pressed our ears to the screen door. Muffled grumbles came from behind the other side, and we took off before he was even close to the door. He sounded more ancient than Miss Mavis!

"Yeah, that's a big 'No' for me," Rose laughed as we skipped away.

"Hey, that one seems more promising," I observed, pointing to a boxy blue two level across the street.

We meandered up to the front door and Rose knocked again.

"Just a minute!" a friendly voice called out. And then the telltale click of a cane started knocking down the hallway.

"Nope, not this one either," Rose called as we jogged off.

Over the next hour or so, we excused ourselves from house after house. One of our knocks started a chorus of several screaming children, and another revealed an already present wife. The fourth one, a grey boxcar-style, had a putrid and pungent front porch and its neighbor had beer bottles stacked high up under the windowsill. All the others in between featured generally crotchety or unpleasant sounding residents. We strolled between each home, leisurely and confident, getting comfortable with our ability to say no.

"These are all duds," Rose mused as we walked along the central path of the neighborhood. "Let's try going this way," she suggested, motioning towards a small fork in the road. Choosing the left side took you right back to the beginning, a big loop around the neighborhood. The right side, however, led down a small hill and into a new corner of the town. A corner we had yet to visit.

Tromping down the slope, I counted only twelve houses in this newer section of the neighborhood. One boxcar-style cottage stood out as particularly well manicured. It was buttercream yellow and had six red geraniums planted out front, not a weed in sight. Two small windows framed the front door, which was attached to a tidy porch with a chair neatly tucked in the corner. Whoever lived there clearly cared about appearances.

"Ok," Rose whispered, "what do you think about this next one?"

"A cat person," I predicted. "*Lots* of cats." We giggled and moseyed up the neatly edged sidewalk.

A shiny new mailbox greeted us as we strolled the mint-lined walkway to the house. Red and white checkered curtains hung inside the windows that faced in our direction and some gardening tools sat carefully off to the side, stacked perfectly one on top of the other. As we took the three steps up to the front porch, we both caught a whiff of that new paint smell. Right as Rose's fist reached forward to knock, a man opened the door.

"Actually, I think we might be lookin' for you."

The door opened so abruptly that we didn't have a chance to run away even if we wanted to. We froze like the mannequins we had seen in the downtown storefronts, albeit less glamorous looking.

"Well hello there," he mused, taking in the sight before him.

Rose and I looked at each other and then back at him. We hadn't gotten this far before. This wasn't part of the game. I tried to say hello in return, but my tongue felt fat and heavy. He was tall and young, maybe early 20s, and dressed in a clean, perfectly pressed white shirt with pleated tan slacks. He had a thin, tan mustache that was the same shade as his sandy hair. Most people would call him handsome, but something about his eyes caught me off guard. They seemed nervous, on edge, the hazel center tinged with pink. Darting back and forth from me to Rose, they finally settled on her. They narrowed as his thin lips shaped into a small smile. Rose cleared her throat and nudged me with her elbow.

"Oh! Yeah. Um, hi," I responded, but nothing else came out.

"Hi," he repeated slowly, encouraging us to respond. Biting the side of his mouth, he crossed his arms and leaned against the door frame. "Are you two ladies lost? I haven't seen you around and you seem a bit," his hand circled in the air, "confused."

"Not lost," my words finally came back to me. "Actually, I think we might be lookin' for you. Can we come in?" I looked at Rose and she nodded and shrugged. Relief washed over me knowing that I hadn't let her down yet.

His eyebrows jumped up in surprise, but he responded as politely as he could. "Of course, of course," he answered. "We pride ourselves on hospitality around here." He pushed the screen door open and held it out of our way, motioning for us to enter.

"Please, come on in. I'm Russ," he greeted as he put out his hand to shake ours.

"I'm Ivy and this is my big sister, Rose," I replied, reciprocating the handshake.

"Oh please, allow me," he drawled as he took Mama's carpet bag off of Rose's shoulder.

Stepping inside his house was like stepping inside a painting of a house. Everything was tidy, orderly, and clean. Almost too clean, especially compared to our home. There were no signs of anyone else living there, and it smelled slightly off, almost like it had been sanitized. Like he had been trying to cook, but ended up burning something, and then tried to cover that up with cleanser.

The narrow entryway opened up to a small dining area with a table setting for four, and the rest of the house grew out to our left. We followed Russ down a hallway that seemed to be the spine of the home and passed the kitchen on our left. There was a single plate and a frying pan sitting on the counter, otherwise the room was spotless. After the kitchen, we passed a bathroom on our right, then a closed door which I presumed was the bedroom, and then finally a sunny sitting room opened up at the end.

"Have a seat," he motioned, showing us to a green and yellow floral sofa in the last room. "Can I get you anything to drink? I'm afraid I burned the last of my supper and need to go to the market, but I have water and tea."

"Tea would be great," Rose answered. I was so delighted to hear her speak up that I gave her an audible smack on the back.

"Ok, two teas. Be right back, madames," he said, pretending to bow and then disappearing back down the hallway. The room smelled like lemon and vinegar.

"What do you think?" I whispered to Rose. "We can run right now, no questions asked."

She took a slow, controlled inhale through her nose. "No, I think this might work," she speculated. She stared straight ahead, but sounded confident and sure.

"We can't keep runnin'," she continued. "I need to find somethin' suitable. I've been hopin' we might find someone like this."

She turned to face me and grabbed one of my hands, squeezing it in hers. "I'm ready. Now we need to see if he's even interested," she added with a half smile and a roll of her eyes. I hadn't fully processed that part. How hard would it be to find a stranger willing to get himself into this situation?

We knew this was bizarre for us, but hadn't considered it from the man's point of view. Who would sign up for such a strange deal?

She broke her gaze with me, but I kept staring at her. I wanted to look through her. To see if this was what she was actually comfortable with, what she was willing to settle for. To make sure she was telling me the truth. She sat up tall, her shoulders pressed back and her hair tucked behind her ears. Her cheekbones were strong and high, and she looked every bit the star of the show. She was so much older than she was back home, and I believed her. It seemed as right as it could feel, so I nodded and gave her a quick hug as he walked back in.

"Three sweet teas." He handed us our drinks and then settled into a gold sitting chair directly across from us.

"So," he cleared his throat. "You're lookin' for me? Long lost family maybe? Did cousin Iggy do somethin' out of line again?"

"Um, no. We don't know Iggy," I started. "See, we're from several towns over, and we've been on a journey lookin' for someone." He nodded along and leaned back in his chair while he listened. Despite the fact that I was the one speaking, he kept his eyes fixed on Rose.

"We're tryin' to find...See, this is Rose. I already told you that. She's my sister. And...well my Pops has lots of us, four boys plus us, and —."

"I'm lookin' for a husband," Rose declared, so clearly and boldly that I think my shock was greater than Russ's.

"It's time for me to leave home."

"Oh. I see," he considered, setting his glass down on a white crocheted doily. "And you think I might be that person?" The corners of his mouth curved into an amused smirk as he leaned back in his chair and clasped his hands behind his head.

"Maybe," Rose answered. "I don't need much. I'm a good helper and a great cook. I'm lookin' for someone that is kind and clean, and who can offer a bit of money in return. I know the mine's been good 'round here." She brushed her skirt off and raised her chin a little higher.

She was so much more grown and confident than she had been only two short days earlier. It was like the whole crowd from Economy Hall was cheering her on, but only she could hear them this time. A private show that was for her and no one else. She had found her own crown. My gaze flitted back and forth between them as I held my breath and wondered what would happen next.

"Well that is an interestin' proposal, Miss Rose," Russ purred, picking his tea back up. "How old are you?"

"Seventeen, in a few weeks."

He nodded and chewed on his bottom lip. "Is this somethin' you want to do?"

"It is," Rose answered without hesitation, like she had no questions in her mind. "It's time for me to leave home and I want to be smart and intentional about it."

"Well, I have to say that I would love some help and company, and I think you'd come to like me after some time," he replied, smiling at her.

It was happening. This is what we set out to do, but it was surreal to see it unfolding. After all the miles walked, the meals shared, the tears and smiles and friends and stories, we were at the end. My heart was both grateful and heavy at the same time. I had not wanted any of this to happen, yet suddenly I didn't want it to end. Sitting in that room and watching this transaction, I felt like I wasn't supposed to be there.

"I do, too." Rose paused and cleared her throat. "Is there anythin' you can offer my family?" she asked, without a doubt or worry in her voice.

Still leaning back in his chair, he now crossed his arms over his chest and released a noise that was part grunt and part laugh. "You were right about the mine doin' well."

He got up and drifted across the room to a thin cherry cabinet that had an oil lamp sitting on top, also perched on a doily. It had a small drawer, and when he opened it I could see an envelope inside. He pulled out several bills with a 20 stamped on them. Never in my life had I seen a bill that big, let alone a handful of them.

"This would likely be a pleasin' amount to bring home to your family," he boasted, handing the bills to me. There were five of them.

I looked at Rose and she gave me a genuine, proud smile. "I think that sounds good," she nodded.

An awkward silence descended over the room as we alternated between looking at each other and the floor. As much as my body, heart, and brain were fighting it, I could sense that it was time for me to go. I just couldn't bring myself to initiate it.

"Well, I s'pose I should walk you out," Rose gulped.

"Oh!" Russ countered. "I'm sure it's been a long morning, you're more than welcome to stay for a night or two."

I looked at Rose, the pit in my stomach growing. She stared back blankly, neither one of us knowing how to do this part.

"Thanks," I choked, "but I gotta get back to my Pops. Not sure how he's doin' without us, ya know?" I rubbed the back of my neck, a pain starting to build in my head. Rose nodded and stared at her feet.

"Suit yourself, you know how to find us if you need to," he responded.

Russ waved goodbye, but remained comfortably seated in his chair, feet propped up on the coffee table. Pop told us that a man always gets up when a lady enters or leaves a room, but I didn't want to ruin anything by calling that to his attention. I waved and dragged myself to the front door with Rose. When I looked over my shoulder one last time, he winked at me. Angry butterflies started flitting through my stomach and chest.

My brain had completely blocked out the end of our story. We had slept next to each other every single night for our whole wide lives, shared every type of moment that people could share. We had danced around the fire while Pop played the washboard, and cried together when we missed Mama. We had pieced together every slipshod meal you can imagine, and performed on stage at the swankiest jazz bar in New Orleans. It wasn't that Rose was a big part of my life, Rose *was* my life. How I would go on without her was a mystery to me.

I wrapped my arms around her waist and hugged her as tight as my body could manage, fearing that it might be the last time. I smelled in her smells and tried to absorb everything about her body as her arms held me tight. She finally, gently, broke our hold and held me by my shoulders. My tears had soaked the front of her dress, but she seemed calm and focused. Resolute. That moment was the hardest moment of my life.

"I'll be fine," she promised, wiping my nose with her hem. "And I'll write. Remember, this is what we planned on."

I nodded vigorously. As selfish as it was, I could only think about myself in that moment. I felt like my life was ending and I didn't know how to cope with it.

"Take care of the boys. Tell them I'm good and not to worry. Come visit whenever you want," she reassured. "You already know the way." Words had completely failed me, so I just kept nodding. I felt like a complete failure for making this part so messy and miserable.

"We knew this would happen, now it's time to do it," she repeated. I buried my head into her chest as she stroked my hair. "I love you, Ivy. Thank you."

"I don't why you're thankin' me," I spit out between sobs. "All I'm doin' is makin' this worse."

"No!" she exclaimed, pushing me away so she could look at me. "You have turned this into an adventure! Without you we'd have never gotten up on stage. Never woulda eaten jambalaya 'til we exploded. Without you?" She shook her head, her eyes now filled with tears.

"Ivy, without you, life would hardly be worth living. You make *everything* better."

****

We sat on the porch steps for a while longer, remembering the food, music, and new friends that we had encountered on our journey. The sun tickled the treetops, blocking some of its light and cooling down the afternoon heat.

"If you ever need to, you just run straight home," I instructed her. "No questions asked, just come on home."

She smiled at me and added, "And if *you* ever need to, you just run straight *here*. No questions asked." She wrapped me up in one last hug.

Rose stepped back and blew a kiss to me, then did a little Charleston for good measure. She knew that I wouldn't be able to hold back a smile. My boldness has always been labeled as strength, but in that moment I wished to be as strong as my sweet, quiet Rose.

The screen door slowly creaked closed, then slammed louder than I expected, jolting me back into the present. I stood there, feet glued to the soil, watching my big sister step into a new life neither of us knew about. She blew another kiss and waved as I watched her turn away from me.

I stayed there for several moments. Flashbacks popped into my brain that I hadn't expected, like the time we borrowed the neighbor's deep, cast iron pot to make beignets. And another one from when Reed stole a half gallon of peroxide from Crazy David and we all bleached our hair. Memories from our childhood. From our life. From when we were inseparable, together forever.

The sun was now behind the treetops, and I forced myself to turn around and start walking. It was time to make the long journey back. I breathed in a deep lungful of Rose's new home, and turned back up the pathway. The familiar beat of dirt kicking up under my feet resumed, and I began calculating about how long it would take to get back home. And whether or not Mr. Sebastian would let me stay at The Magnolia again. I thought about Miss Lucille and wondered if she would remember me, and how many details I would share with Pop versus how many I would share with Miss Mavis. I was at the end of his long windy walkup when Rose's scream shattered the silence.

"We gotta go baby, we gotta run."

Have you ever had one of those nightmares where you need to run away, but you are cemented to the ground? Like a bad guy is chasing you and you can't escape, no matter how hard you try? No matter how deep you dig? Running to Rose, trying to reach her after that scream felt just like that, except it was real.

My feet pounded the ground as quickly as they could, tossing dust in every direction, but I couldn't get to her fast enough. As hard as I ran, it seemed like I was staying in place. The front door was about three hundred feet away, but it may as well have been in New York. And my sister was on the other end, in desperate trouble. I tossed my bag onto the ground as soon I heard her, I wasted no time in turning around and sprinting towards the house, but it still wasn't fast enough. No one deserved this, but especially not Rose.

I charged straight into the screen door with all my speed behind me, but rather than feeling it fly open, a sharp pain shot through my wrists. It was locked. It was no accident; he had planned this. He knew exactly what he was doing and he locked me out. We had been speaking straight to a monster and didn't even know it. How could we have learned so much and still not noticed an enemy right under our noses?

I grabbed the door handle with both hands and shook it so hard I thought it would rip right off the hinges, but it didn't budge. Rose's muffled yell seeped through the walls, indistinct and pleading. His voice was audible too, but I couldn't make out any words. Just deep, angry babbling.

"Rose!" I yelled as loud as I could, so that she would know I was there. "Rose, I'm comin'! I'm right here Rose!" I banged on the window right next to the door, but that didn't budge either.

The door seemed an impossible option and my time was running short. I thought about running to a neighbor's house, but that might take too long. And what if no one was home? What if they didn't believe me? I knew that I was Rose's only option. I had to figure this out.

I looked around for any sort of tool to help me get inside and then remembered the pile of garden supplies we had noticed when we first walked up. I sprinted over and grabbed a small shovel. Running back up the porch, I used the sharp corner to cut the screen on the front door. Reaching through the hole in the screen, I unlocked the door from the inside. My hands trembled and I fumbled for a second, but finally unlatched the handle. Shoving the door open, I tumbled back into the dining room we first visited only moments ago.

"Rose!" I called out, my voice sounding scared and strained. It didn't even sound like mine as it echoed through the empty house.

I expected to see something horrific, bloodstains or a murder scene, but there was no sign of either of them. It was completely silent and empty, like the whole thing had been in my head. Had it been? Was I losing my mind so quickly after leaving her? My heavy breathing filled the entire house, like it was pulsing all around me, moving the walls in and out with each inhale and exhale. Tiptoeing down the hallway, feeling both terrified and fearless, I rounded the corner into the sitting room when I saw her. Rose was on the ground, bent like a broken doll. Her arm stuck out in an unnatural way, like she had fallen, and the top of her dress was slightly ripped. The air completely evaporated from my lungs, like the entire room was in a vacuum. It felt like all of Louisiana was stuck in a tube with no oxygen going in or out.

I lunged forward. "Rose," I pleaded, patting her cheek. "Rose, open your eyes, I'm so sorry I left you." Big fat tears poured onto her chest as I tried to shake her awake.

Panic and urgency shoved my sorrow and pity out of the way. "We gotta get you outta here," I said, blinking the tears away so that I could see straight again. I stood up and grabbed her feet, determined to drag her outside and seek help once we were safe again, out in the open. Without any warning, an overwhelming force grabbed me from behind. Like a magnet was peeling me away from my sister's limp body. Russ had one arm around my neck in a headlock and the other gripped both of my wrists behind my back. I could barely breathe.

"You stupid girls," he hissed into my ear. "What did you think was gonna happen? Think anyone's gonna miss you?" His voice sounded like sand. His mustache brushed against my cheek. Though I hadn't noticed it earlier, I now smelled the stench of whiskey on his breath. I kicked both my feet as hard as I could, trying to land something that would do some damage, but I was no match for him.

"Her, I'm going to keep," he growled. "But you? I'll just bury you in the backyard. No one'll find you here, swamp rat."

What had I done? How had I let this happen? He stumbled slightly, loosening his grip on my wrists and I seized the moment, swinging my arms around as hard as I could. All I needed to do was land one good punch, but my strength was fading as his grip around my neck tightened like a vice. The house started to spin and throb, and my peripheral vision turned dark and fuzzy, like when you stand up too fast. I stretched my legs as long as they could go, but my toes barely grazed the ground. I could tell that he was dragging me away somewhere, but my body couldn't do anything about it. He was too strong and I was too little. Far smaller than I had ever imagined.

Darkness bled into the center of my vision, making a black tunnel. When I looked up, I saw Pops standing there. He was calling me over to a crawfish boil with fried green tomatoes. The boys smiled at me and I could almost smell their long johns after a day in the mine. Rose skipped ahead and called me to her, ready to jump off the pier into the bayou. As I ran to her, Miss Mavis stepped into view with a tray of freshly baked cookies, her radio playing Louis Armstrong over the familiar click-clack that characterized her living room. Miss Lucille and Gilbert joined in and he put an arm around her, smiling and laughing while MJ and Bobbie danced for us. I smiled back at them, happy just to have them by my side as the lights went down.

And then I heard it. A noise I will never forget in all my years on Earth. A strange and crackling sound. A sickly, disturbing crunch that sounded strangely biological. Like a million eggshells going through a meat grinder. And right after the noise, almost immediately, I could breathe again. I gasped for air as my loved ones vaporized from sight, waving and cheering me on. Was I dead? Was the crack the sound of me getting slingshotted up to Heaven?

A heavy, blurry voice called out to me. "You ok? You ok I? We gotta go baby, we gotta run." It was Rose. Her voice sounded distorted, but I knew it was her. I blinked hard and saw her crouched next to me. We were still in the house, in his empty dining room, not far from the front door. Russ was sprawled on his back only inches away. Rose had a firm grip on the frying pan I had noticed when we first walked in.

I nodded, shaking off the fog as reality quickly settled in. Rose helped me to my feet, then grabbed Mama's carpet bag. We took a few steps towards the door and I could already sense my strength coming back to me.

"Wait," she blurted, jumping over Russ and running into the sitting room. "Rose!" I cried. If he woke up, he would be between us. I grabbed the frying pan that had just been in her hands and held it like a baseball bat.

"What are you doing? We gotta get outta here!" I pleaded. My head was pounding and tears started sliding down my nose. We needed to leave that house. Forever. I kept my eyes locked on Russ's body, worried that he would spring back to life. But fear no longer dominated my thoughts. Now I was angry.

She reappeared, stepping quickly but carefully over the unconscious demon on the ground, and stuffed an envelope into her bag. We were at the screen door, our hands on the handle, when we both paused and turned around.

"Go to Hell," Rose spit at him. We fled up the dirt path and didn't look back.

"What do we do now?"

You never know what you're capable of until you're forced to figure it out. Once we left that house, we ran longer than either of us had ever run in our lives, silently keeping up with one another, step for step. Adrenaline coursed through our bodies and we were well out of that town before we slowed to a walk. Sweat soaked through the back of my overalls, but I finally felt my heart rate calm down.

"Do you think he's dead?" I asked her.

Rose shook her head. "I don't know, I."

I wanted to slow down even more, but her pace was still sharp and urgent.

"Honestly, I don't care," she continued.

Old Rose would have already said that whatever happened had been her fault. Would have taken the blame and held it silently with her for all her days. But not this new Rose, not the one that had started blooming the last few days. She was tough and had some thorns that she hadn't known about before. New Rose understood that she was beautiful and worthy, proud and powerful.

"What happened?" I asked her. "I was almost at the road when I heard you scream."

Our feet kicked up gravel as we kept a brisk, steady pace. Rose's eyes stayed locked on the blank space in front of her.

"He was a bad man. He tried to hurt me," she stated, cold and serious. She cleared her throat. "He would've hurt me if you hadn't been there." And then she stopped and looked right at me.

"You saved me, Ivy," she said, her voice shaking. I wrapped her up in a hug, so completely overjoyed that she was standing next to me. To be alive and healthy had never felt so wonderful before. Tears of both fear and gratitude started flowing out of each of us, our bodies and hearts tired.

"You saved me, too," I heaved. "I would've died there, at some point. I know it."

We were overcome with joy, realizing that we were both together and okay, and we started laughing and sobbing happy tears. Tears of relief. You ever been in one of those situations where you're feeling so many different things that you just start to laugh? Not like it's actually funny, but like your body doesn't know what else to do? Well that was what happened to us, and before we knew it we were both cracking up on the side of the road.

We resumed our journey, recounting every detail.

"How'd you get inside? I watched him lock the door!"
"I used some of his gardening tools to cut the screen!"

"When did you wake up? Did you plan on usin' the fryin' pan, or did you just notice it?"

"I just grabbed the first heavy-lookin' thing I could find!"

"What else did he say to you?"

"That you'd never remember the way back and no one would be able to find me again."

And then I asked the bigger question. "So...what do we do now?"

With her chin up high and a knowing smirk on her face, Rose answered me as though she had no questions in the world - "What we shoulda done all along."

"Excuse me?" I paused and cocked my head to the side. "What in the world should we have done all along?"

She shot me a sly wink and then kept walking. This newfound confidence was both inspiring and frustrating to keep up with.

"Rose!" I yelled at her, running to catch back up. "I didn't come all the way out here to be left in the dark! What the heck kinda plan do you have?"

"I took more of his money so I know I can make it work," she reassured herself. I figured that was what she had gone back into the sitting room for.

"Make *what* work?" I asked.

She stopped, drinking in a great big breath. "I'm goin' to Chicago." She flashed an I-can't-believe-I-just-said-that-aloud smile and nodded her head.

"I know where Gilbert's shows are gonna be, and MJ promised that I'll always have a place in the band if I can get up there." She exhaled deeply, a rosy eagerness filling her chest and cheeks. "I think I can do this."

Without even meaning to, our time in New Orleans came right back to me. The smell of cigar smoke filled my nose and stung my eyes. The warmth of the spotlight as we climbed up on stage. The sound of the audience hooting and hollering for the band. For us. For her. The way Gilbert held her just so when he hugged her goodbye. Rose was right. She could do it.

I looked at her and smiled. "How?"

She grinned and started rambling, talking animatedly with her hands. "The train station. We passed it on the way out of New Orleans, it was just beyond Todd's and Miss Lucille's. I have the money for a ticket now, and Gilbert wrote down their schedule."

"So you could get on the train and meet them at their next show," I finished.

"That's what I was thinkin'," she nodded. I don't know if there is a word in our language for how Rose looked just then. Like she was excited and hopeful, yet also scared and reluctant.

"Maybe you could come with," she suggested, her voice much quieter than it had been only seconds before.

I know she would have liked me to come with, truly. Rose was my very best friend and I know she felt the same way. But I also knew that I was too young, and that Pops and the boys needed me. That night in New Orleans was the best night of my whole wide life, but I couldn't do that everyday. Our mission was to find a new home for Rose, a family. And we did just that. I couldn't think of a better family than Gilbert and the band. I wouldn't have to worry about her anymore.

"I'll visit," I replied. "You know Pop and the boys would starve to death without one of us."

Rose bit her lip and nodded, new tears welling up in her eyes. "I'll write and you can come visit. Be our guest performer." I couldn't help but grin at that. "And you don't need to worry about me now, I'll be right where I'm supposed to be."

"I was thinkin' the same thing."

"Thank you for helpin' me be me."

Union Station was at least four stories tall and made entirely of tan bricks, but as the sun started to set, the amber light made it look like it was pure gold. Like a royal palace with special powers that could take people to all sorts of magical places. Massive archways welcomed visitors and bid farewell to those heading out.

"We've been inside here before," Rose murmured, bringing me back to the present. "When you were really little, maybe two or three. Some uncle from Detroit was comin' down to visit and we picked him up here."

"I don't remember that at all," I thought aloud. "Do you?"

"Yeah, a little," she stood on her tiptoes and craned her neck to look around. "I think you get tickets over this way."

She rushed away and blended into the crowd just like all the other mysterious strangers with somewhere to be. There were so many folks coming and going that it made my head spin. There must have been thousands of people going through that station each day. I remained on my corner of cobblestone as my eyes darted every which way, trying to capture each person who whooshed past me. A young couple threw their heads back and laughed, and I recognized them as the stylish duo from Todd and Lucille's. Another lady strolled by with a shiny black cat poking out of her purse! I had never seen anything like it in my life. She winked at me and made a "ssh" gesture with her finger to her mouth.

"Ivy!" Rose called out, unphased by the crowd.

I turned around and captured what I saw like a photograph in my memory. Amidst the busy platform pulsing with exotic and exciting people coming and going, Rose stole the spotlight for the second time in her life. The lowering sun illuminated her in such a way that it gave her a halo. Standing there with a one-way ticket and her carpet bag at her feet, she smiled so big that it rivaled the moon. But it wasn't just a look of joy, it was deeper than that. It was excited. Proud. Ready. She looked so grown up, like she had aged five years since we first left home. I was staring at a person who knew what she wanted and was ready to go out and take it. She reminded me so much of Bobbie and MJ, and I realized for the first time that she must only be two or three years younger than them. Taking in a deep inhale, I smiled and nodded at her. Words didn't seem like they would be able to capture all my thoughts, wishes, and emotions.

"Here," I put my hand out with the money Russ had given me before I first left. "Use this to find Gilbert. You could probably even buy a new dress or two before you get to-" Before I could finish my thought, Rose wrapped me up in a hug as tight as her arms would let her.

"I will never be able to thank you enough, Ivy," she whispered. "You are the most precious part of my life." Then she held me by the shoulders and looked me in my eyes. "Thank you for bein' you. Thank you for helpin' me be me."

I had so many feelings building up inside me, like a balloon ready to either float away or pop. Like my soul was filling up with sadness and pride and excitement and fear all at the same time. I saw our garden, bursting with late July tomatoes, but no one to pick them with me. I heard Pops playing his old washboard, but no one to dance with me. I smelled the lilies in full bloom, but no one to stop and understand what that meant with me. But I also smelled wine and cigarettes wafting through burning spotlights. I heard the string bass keeping time for everyone in a way that made you feel it through your whole body. I felt the heat of the night getting stuck between all the notes and rhythms. I saw Rose being her best self and living her best life. The balloon burst all at once and tears started pouring down the front of my overalls.

"I'm not sad," I heaved. "I swear, I'm just so happy that you're going. I'm gonna miss you so much." I was back in her arms.

"Ivy, I know you'll be fine. I've never had any doubts about that," Rose confessed. "But I need you to know that I'm gonna be fine, too. More than fine. I'm gonna be who I'm supposed to be. And I will write to you all the time, so you better get some pencils on the way home." She gave me a nudge.

"I know," I cleared my throat and stood up tall again. "Take this." I stuck the money back out.

"I have what I need to get up there and live awhile," she answered. "Bring it to Pops. Pick up a chicken or two when you get close to home again."

We both giggled at the thought of how excited Pops would be at that.

"What should I tell him?" I asked. Did he deserve to know what really happened? So much of this felt sacred to just Rose and me.

"Whatever you want," Rose mused. "I think he'd be happy with the truth."

We stared at each other for another long minute, drinking in our last moment together, when the train next to us let out the biggest whistle I had ever heard. Rose jumped and we both laughed again.

"Get home safe and watch for my letters everyday," she instructed. "When you can leave the boys on their own, come find me." She wrapped me in her arms for the last time.

"All aboard!" the conductor yelled out, and Rose started backing away. Her dress billowed out from the steam engine, carpet bag under her arm and a one way ticket clenched in her fist. Like the star of a movie, the main character who is about to go chase her dream. Someone you can't help but root for and fall in love with.

"Go find Gil and band!" I called out. "Tell 'em I said hi!" People were all around her now as she climbed the steps into the train car. "And make sure you sing loud enough for everyone to hear!" I could see her settle into a window seat as the wheels started to churn.

With my small pack at my feet, I flailed both arms over my head. She smiled and waved back as the train started to pull away.

A sudden burst of worry rushed through me. How could I have been such an idiot? How could I have forgotten? "Wait!" I yelled, running alongside the now chugging train. With my feet pumping below me, I shoved my hand into my pockets trying to find it. I had kept it safe since the morning we left home.

"Ivy you're gonna get run over before we even get out of town!" Rose yelled through the window.

I reached my hand up toward the window as she leaned down, grabbing Mama's lily from my grip. "Take Mama with you! She'll take care of you!" One of her hands clutched the flower, and the other one covered her mouth in surprise. My legs slowed down and I stopped running, but my eyes stayed locked on Rose sitting in her window seat. When she moved her hand away from her face, she was beaming down at me. As she blew me a kiss, I lost sight of her.

"You are her pride and joy, Miss Ivy."

The golden curtain that had floated across downtown New Orleans slipped beneath its own shadows. A few stars vied for attention with the setting sun. Rose's train was now well on its journey north. The air was streaked with a light chill, and while I was comforted by the cooler temperature, it also reminded me of my solo trek back home.

As my feet shuffled through the crowd, my imagination took over and I wondered about Rose's new life. I pictured her pulling into a station ten times bigger than the one we had just left, surrounded by shiny buildings that flirted with the sky. Maybe she would make a friend on the train, and they could explore together and watch out for each other. Images of dress shops, restaurants, and jazz clubs flooded into my mind with such vigor that I could almost touch the silk and taste the spices. I couldn't wait to hear all about it.

My daydreams made the time pass quickly and before I knew it, I was well out of town and back amongst the company of willows and ferns. My senses started to sharpen again as I heard the katydids and crickets singing lullabies. My eyes adjusted to the dark, and I stopped to appreciate the silvery glow that the moon cast over each turn of the landscape. Even in moments of both figurative and literal darkness, we can find the beauty in our lives.

Despite my exhaustion and heartbreak, my brain started buzzing again. As unlikely and impossible as this had once seemed, it now felt like the most perfect resolution to our story. Rose was always capable and worthy of the life she was now beginning, she had just been too contained before. How can you expect a rose to bloom if you keep it in a pot on the windowsill? There is so much greatness inside each of us. Sometimes, we just need the opportunity to explore it.

****

My journey back home had started so late in the day that when I was ready to stop for the night I found myself in the middle of nowhere again, no motels or hostels nearby. Instead of recreating our night in Room 115, I decided to sleep near the quiet waters that trickled out of the bayou. Tromping off of the path towards the river, I found a clearing between the protruding roots of an ancient oak. A perfect nest for the night. I gathered armfulls of Spanish moss and made a little mattress right there on the riverbed. The soft foliage and protective sides made it feel even more comfortable than my bed back home. For the first time since we left, my mind drifted to the boys. Was their new work steady? Were they eating enough? Did they miss me? I nestled into my cozy forest nook and let my eyes relax on the mosaic in the sky.

The stars were so clear that I couldn't have counted them all if I had tried, so I didn't. Instead, I decided that Rose was seeing those same stars as she looked out of her train car window, and that Mama was up there in them.

"Mama," I whispered to her, "thank you. Thank you for makin' me." I had so many other things to say to her, but my body had had enough for one day. I fell asleep before I could put them all to words.

The sun sprinkled rays through the old oak's leaves and tickled me awake.
Thankfully the light breeze from the water was still sighing its way through
the day. It was going to be a hot one. I reached up and stretched from my
fingertips to my toes, not wanting to move from my bed. I had an old roll
from New Orleans, but my stomach was too tumbly to think about that.
Why wasn't I more excited to go home? I willed myself to get up and
splash my face with some cool, fresh water from the brook, but I couldn't
help but feel reluctant to go back. How do you return to normal after an
experience like that? How do you go through life when a part of your heart
has been ripped out? But then I thought of what Rose had faced during our
entire journey. The strength and grit she demonstrated in those few days
was far more than most people would show in their whole wide lives. If
she could get through that, step by step, then I could move forward, too.

Back on the road. Dust kicking up all around my feet. Not another person
in sight. The trees started to morph again, getting shorter and squatter,
cradling the pathway. Ferns and lilies dotted my path, and I noticed the ivy-
covered oak that Rose had pointed out earlier, breaking our first silence. I
was almost home.

****

The familiar screen door swung open and Miss Mavis let out a gaspy
giggle when she saw me. "Well Miss Ivy," she smiled with outreached
arms. "It appears as though you have some stories to tell me."

After fixing some tea and arranging a plate full of gooey butterscotch
cookies, I spent the whole afternoon telling Miss Mavis about our

impossible adventure. She never interrupted once, just listened with wide eyes at each detail and twist. I did my best to tell her just how spicy the jambalaya was, and how big Miss Lucille sounded when she talked. About our Cinderella makeovers, the smells of lipstick and champagne, and our show-stopping performance. I described our knock knock game, and how brave we both were with Russ. About the magical train station and the lonesome journey back. I dug into my bag to show her the headband that MJ let me keep. Her eyes were bigger than a supper plate.

"And so now Rose is on a train to Chicago to find Gil and the band. I think she's probably pullin' in right now if I'm doin' my math right," I ended, wiping the last cookie crumbs from my chin.

"Well," she sighed. "Well well," she whispered, tears building up in her eyes.

"I'm sorry Miss Mavis, I probably shouldn't have told you anything." I felt guilty and stupid for dumping so much on her. "You're just an old lady and all I'm doin' is worryin' you."

"Just an old lady?!" she guffawed, playfully swatting at my shoulder. "No no, Miss Ivy. No," she murmured, shaking her head at me. "I am *not* cryin' because I'm worried."

She sat real still for a few moments, just clearing her throat and looking off in the distance. The familiar click-clack of her rocker calmed and reassured me. I wondered how many conversations she and Mama had shared, how many glasses of sweet tea they had sipped.

"I'm cryin' because I can see how proud Lily would be of you girls," she continued, tears now streaming down her face. I thought about the lily I gave Rose as the train pulled away.

Miss Mavis smiled at me while the tears were still coming down. "You are her pride and joy, Miss Ivy. Tougher than any of the boys." She gave me a fake punch on the arm and I giggled. Nothing could disturb my crown anymore.

"Rose is gonna be great."

Cinnamon and laundry soap lingered in my clothes, and the click-clack of her rocker kept rhythm in my head. I had made that walk home hundreds of times, and yet somehow it was different this time. Shorter and smaller. It seemed more like a casual stroll rather than the big trip that it used to be. I knew the distance itself hadn't changed, just my perspective on it.

The path started to look and smell like home. Willows and wet sand and little lizards. While the air in New Orleans was still wet and humid, it had nothing on the thick, sticky air of home. Had it always been like that? It felt harder to breathe than it had before we left. And I swear there was more water than before - it was absolutely everywhere. Along the walkways, flooding up from the creeks, even pooled around the base of the trees. My brain knew that it had always been that way, but it was almost like I had never seen it before. Or that maybe I had seen it, but I hadn't really looked at it. I wondered what kinds of places Rose could see from the train. Did Chicago have bayous? Was the air like ours? Were there any buildings as nice as The Magnolia? I couldn't wait to get her first letter.

"Ivy?" My eyes came back into focus and my visions of Rose's adventures vaporized right in front of me. Reed stood in the middle of the path, only fifty yards or so in front of me. "Ivy!" he called out, running towards me at full speed. "Ivy! Are you ok?" He wrapped me up in a big hug and kept asking me questions, although I was so surprised to see him that none of the words were sticking with me. I couldn't remember the last time he had hugged me.

I couldn't help but smile. "Put me down, you fool!" I giggled at him. He looked younger than I thought he had a few days earlier. "I brought this home," I exclaimed, slinging a bag with a chicken at him. After I left Miss Mavis, I made one last stop to get some food, paper, and pencils.

"Holy Moses I'm so glad you're home," he sighed, grinning and still hanging onto me. "I started to get so worried. I hated myself for letting you go. We all did." He nervously ran his hand through his thick, wavy hair. "But here you are. All in one piece, plus a chicken," he chuckled. "No surprises there." I always knew I could do it, but now he did, too.

As relieved as I was to see him, part of me took him to be a stranger. Like I had lived such a different life in the past three days that maybe he didn't know me anymore. During the quiet journey back, my imagination entertained itself with stories about Rose's future. I pictured her practicing with MJ and Bobbie, getting their harmonies just so. I envisioned her onstage, right behind Gilbert, and then celebrating with everyone afterwards. My body could hardly hold it all in. But now, being back at home, back with my brothers and the promise of life as it was before, my heart was flooded with sadness and a longing for her that I knew could never be filled again. Reed was so happy to see me that I felt awful for experiencing anything but joy and gratitude for being back with the family that loves me. I mustered up a smile and we started walking towards our shack.

"So what's been goin' on? How's the new job?" I asked.

"It's pretty good. A lot cleaner than the old one," he smiled, showing me his charcoal-free hands. "Gosh we've missed you though, Ivy." He paused. "So uh, how did everything go? I mean…" he stammered. He desperately wanted to know how Rose's story had turned out, but didn't know how to ask about it.

"It was fine," I stated, smiling back. "Rose is real happy."

****

"My little weed!" Pops wrapped me up and spun me around like a ragdoll. I laughed and squealed like a little kid again. I had missed him more than I thought I would. No matter how conflicted I may have been, I would always be happy when Pops gave me love and attention. It was good to be home.

"And look what she brought," Reed announced, thumping the chicken onto the table. Everyone cheered and took turns slapping me on the back.

"Alright get outta my way and let me cook this thing!" I teased them. Our little home, the deteriorating shack that raised us, felt so much emptier without Rose, but somehow smaller at the same time. Before we left, I always looked at home as home. But now, I looked at the wooden floors and thought of the tiles at our hotel. I looked at the bare windows and thought of the velvet curtains at Economy Hall. Our family's two communal mattresses made me think of Room 115. But I also saw us kids playing jacks out in the lawn and dancing late into the night. Crawfish boils and Kick the Can. The way we feel about home and family is never straightforward, I suppose. Maybe that's part of growing up. You add layers to all your feelings.

No one asked about Rose, other than Reed on the pathway. I think they all knew it must have turned out alright if I came back safely without her. Maybe all this was harder on them than I had given them credit for. Miss Mavis would probably say that they didn't want to talk about it because that makes it more real.

We had a delicious, boisterous dinner all together, a real feast full of good food and even better conversation. My chicken turned out juicy and flavorful, and the garden was full of okra and tomatoes that hadn't been picked since we left. It wasn't Todd and Miss Lucille's jambalaya, but it was a showstopper on its own. I asked them all about their new jobs in the quarry and they could hardly get through a story without cracking up. Apparently, the first day on the job, Ever had slipped and slid all the way down a deep canyon of gravel.

"He couldn't get back up because it was like grease," Pops roared. He had tears building up in the corners of his eyes. "It took him half an hour to get himself back out! The foreman almost charged him for lost time." Ever blushed and tried to explain his side of the story, but everyone kept teasing and shushing him.

Pop told the boys to clean up and then turned to me. "Ivy, can you help me pick some of these cucumbers out here? We got more than we can keep up with."

We walked outside together and a nice warm breeze coming in from the bayou greeted us. The tomato leaves made the whole air smell fresh and the lilies shone in the moonlight. I really did miss this.

"You're ok, Ivy?" Pops asked as we walked towards the cucumber vines.

"Yeah Pop, I'm fine," I smiled. I still hadn't decided how much to share with him. How could I possibly explain everything and do it justice? It occurred to me that if he asked for the details, I would tell him. I had nothing to hide. At the same time, if he didn't ask, I liked the idea of keeping our adventure sacred.

"And I did real good with this part," I bragged. I reached into the front of my overalls and gave him the five crinkled bills from Russ. He inhaled slowly and closed his eyes so tight that I could see all the wrinkles near his temples. He put it in his pocket and looked down at the ground.

"I woulda just died if something had happened to you," he whispered. "Either of you. As soon as you left I couldn't believe I let it happen." We listened to bullfrogs gossiping to one another.

"I'm just real happy you're back," he gushed, putting his arm around me. "And Rose? Reed said she's alright?"

I took a deep breath and looked up at the sky. A shooting star streaked through the deep blue blanket overhead.

"Yeah Pop," I reassured him. "Rose is gonna be great."

****

After dinner, we sat outside and played music late into the night. Ash had gotten really good at the spoons, and Pop got out his harmonica. Whether we were dancing around the crackling campfire or playing one of our makeshift instruments, it was clear that we were all happy and relieved. It was a joyful night of music and laughter.

Eventually, our music quieted as the exhaustion from quarry work and a long journey caught up to us. Fireflies were the ones dancing now. The boys started heading inside to bed, Fern first, but I stayed outside watching the embers of the fire glow yellow and orange.

"Ivy girl, I can't keep my eyes open another second," Pop muttered. "Come on in to bed."

"Soon Pops," I reassured him. Despite my exhaustion, I wasn't quite ready to go inside yet.

He smiled and shook his head, then gave me a squeeze around the shoulders from behind. While I would always be his baby, I think he realized how I had grown in the past week.

Sitting outside and listening to the familiar sounds of my life and home, a new peace washed over me. As much as my heart ached over Rose's absence, my love and pride for her was ten times stronger. I missed her and I wanted her next to me, but she was right where she deserved to be. Tears started to flow again as the fire crackled at my feet.

By the time I quietly snuck through the screen door and tiptoed to my side of the cot, the boys were all snoring. I couldn't help but giggle to myself as I thought of this as our own special concert. I curled up in the corner of our mattress, even though I didn't need to share it anymore. I would always sleep on my side. Cradling MJ's headband in my hands, I sank deep into my pillow. The days of walking and singing and fighting and crying all hit me at once. Taking a slow, deep breath, I rolled over and saw her. Rose was standing only a few feet in front of me, waving for me to come closer.

"Follow me!" she called, beaming. I ran to catch up as she pushed open a heavy door in front of us. Cigar smoke and the smell of sweet bourbon hit me almost as hard as the sound of the drums. Rose was running now, her hand outstretched for me, but I couldn't quite catch her. The surrounding crowd was cheering for us, and Miss Mavis was in the front row. Pops stood next to her, smiling and clapping more than anyone else. The heat of the spotlight warmed our faces as we stepped to the front of the stage. Gilbert strolled out from behind the thick velvet curtains, put his hand out to us, and smiled.

www.ingramcontent.com/pod-product-compliance
Lightning Source LLC
Chambersburg PA
CBHW030323160726
47992CB00005B/2132